STRIP MALL

STORIES

MATTHEW THOMAS MEADE

TP

TAILWINDS PRESS

Tailwinds Press
P.O. Box 2283, Radio City Station
New York, NY 10101-2283
www.tailwindspress.com

Published in the United States of America
ISBN: 979-8-9886903-2-0
1st ed. 2023

Strip Mall

For Jenny

CONTENTS

THE SOUTHWEST'S MOST DANGEROUS BABIES

This is a story about a snake, but it isn't the one you're thinking of. The one about the woman nursing the snake back to health who then gets bit and she is like, "Why?" and the snake is all like, "Cuz I'm a fuckin rattlesnake!!!" This is a totally different story. One that has a completely different lesson from that well-known fable.

The snake situation that me and Ty got ourselves into was a whole different thing altogether. It was Ty's fault we got into that circumstance to begin with but what else would you expect from Ty? That boy is just obsessed with danger. Who knows what happened to him that made him that way. I mean, I know some of the things that happened to him. But not all the things.

It wasn't one hundred percent his fault, tho. It was partly my fault. I'm the one who can't sleep unless it's absolutely pitch-black dark. So dark you can't see the hand in front of your face. Dark like the edges of an old painting. Dark like the crawlspace under Nonnie's house after she died. Dark like the trunk of a 1988 Chevy Cavalier. And so since I need it so freaking dark, since I'm the one who made us hang the blanket over the window so there wouldn't even be a sliver of streetlight in the room where we slept, I'm partly to blame. I'm the one who wouldn't let him bring his computer in because I wanted to keep the red and green and yellow lights from flickering across the room like little, quivering traffic signals. I'm the one who made it like that. And, before you ask, yes I know exactly what happened that made me this way, thank you very much.

But it was Ty's decision to get the snake. That's totally on him. That's his fault all the way. Like I said, that boy is obsessed with danger. And with being wild. He used to like to get high and mess around (tho we don't do that anymore on account of what happened last December), to stand near the edges of buildings, and canyons (if he could find one), push buttons of people whose buttons shouldn't be pushed. All that kind of thing.

And it's not like the snake was cheap, either. We probably should have spent the money on rent. Or the electrical bill. Or on food. Or to fix his tattoo. But we didn't. We spent it on a snake. And by "we," I mean Ty.

We had agreed to get a pet though. We didn't say what kind of pet, but we said we would get one. We were getting it because of what had happened in December. I mean, Ty and me didn't talk about that part of it, but that's totally why we were getting it. That much was obvious to me. The only reason we didn't say it outright was because we had agreed never to talk about what happened ever again. And so we didn't.

I was thinking we'd get a hamster or a mouse or a frog, or something ugly like that. Something small and easy that we could pick a name for. Something we would have that would belong to the both of us. Something that Ty and me could both love. Anyway, that's what I was thinking when we decided we should get it.

The next day Ty came home with the rattlesnake, carried the aquarium all the way up three flights of stairs with his scrawny-ass arms. He was groaning and straining as he hefted it up onto the bookshelf that didn't have any books on it anymore. I didn't know he was gonna come home with a snake, but what was I gonna do? It was his place and he was nice enough to let me stay there. Plus he let me name it.

I went with Sammy because Ty never bothered to ask the guy he bought it off if it was a girl snake or a boy snake and Sammy was a nice name for either. Ty heard that you could find out the sex if you measured the distance between their vents and their rattles, but our snake was too young to even have rattles. Instead there was just what Ty said was called a "button" which was a little bump of keratin that collected on the tip of the tail—it was so white it was almost pink and it looked hard, like a little, plastic pen top. Ty said you could also check for a penis that retracted up into their body but neither of us dared to do that. We usually just defaulted to calling the snake a he when we talked tho. Isn't that what most people do?

When I was feeling a bit naïve I'd think that maybe Ty got the thing to give us both some purpose once we decided to give up drinking and pills and all that. To have something that would motivate us and give us some kind of responsibility to something else. I wanted to believe that his sponsor had told him to use it as some kind of sobriety exercise, but other times I knew better. Other times I knew that was all bullshit.

Other times I would admit to myself that the real

reason he bought the rattlesnake was just so he could tap on the glass and make it hiss at him. The real reason he wanted it to hiss at him was so he could hiss back at it. He got it so he could drop frogs and hamsters into the glass aquarium, snickering as he doomed the small creatures, laughing at me as I begged him not to.

"Can't we just feed him snake food?" I asked as he dangled a live mouse over the glass tank, the snake coiling up and making itself dangerous.

"This is snake food, stupid," he would say and drop the living animal into the aquarium. By the time the mouse's legs stopped kicking I would have stopped crying, wiped away my tears, and calmed myself down enough to call the snake my sweet little hunter.

"He's really good at it," I would say as I blew my nose, knowing that anyone, even I, could catch a mouse in a 15" x 10" x 10" area, but not caring because it was our snake and so I loved it. And it was just a little baby too, and so that made me love it even more, tho Ty said that made it more dangerous.

"The babies are the most deadly," he would say, proud of the snake for being lethal, proud of himself for possessing it. "They can't regulate their venom so if you get bit by a baby they give you the full dose."

He loved that. He smiled that half sweet, half evil grin he had, the smile he smiled when we first started sneaking into Quigly's together and he would reach over the bar to grab us beers while the fat bartender flirted with some bimbo with a big chest.

"A baby'll kill you dead if it bites you," he would say, shaking his head wistfully, sucking on his second-to-last clove cigarette. "They just can't control themselves."

I think Ty saw the snake as his special project or something. He thought about it all the time, talked about it all the time. He kept moving the aquarium. First he moved it from the living room to our room, then to the desk near the bed, and finally to the small shelf right next to where we slept. I objected every time but I always caved and would end up cooing at the snake and making love-eyes at it, admonishing Ty every time he would make a monster face at it or agitate the snake in some other Ty-like way. He was a younger brother and so needed to make his presence known, show his dominance in demonstrable ways, get attention any way he could.

He tried to tone all that stuff down after what happened last December, but he wasn't doing a very good job. It wasn't his fault, tho. That's just how he was.

My sponsor told me drinking wasn't about alcohol. That it was a spiritual disease. That drinking was a symptom, just like lashing out, being passive-aggressive, cowardly, or mean. That I needed to examine the source of my disease if I wanted to fix the problem inside me.

"Nothing changes if nothing changes," I've heard many a 12-stepper say.

I don't know if that's true, but any time I told anyone at a meeting that I wasn't sure about something, they would just tell me that I was in the right place and that I should keep coming back.

The night the aquarium broke Ty had been having a dream about being beat up by his older brother. He had been dreaming of the little ballpeen fists coming down and chipping away at him and when he kicked his leg he wasn't trying to set the snake free in our bedroom, but trying to evade the assault his dream brother was waging upon him.

"Sammy," I said when I heard the glass of the aquarium crack as it met the floor. I called the snake by his name, tho admittedly not pronouncing it the way we usually did, with about five extra Ss to approximate the sound a snake makes: Sssssssssammy.

We only did that when we were being sweet and silly and there wasn't any room for that on the night this all happened. We knew as soon as we woke up that we were in too much trouble for being goofy and fun and carefree. When this happened we were both dead-ass screaming our heads off, banging on the walls, trying to get the neighbors to wake up, but they didn't hear us. They never seemed to hear us, even when we were messing around real loud or smashing beer bottles against the walls. Maybe they were deaf? Or dead? Or just liked to listen to us scream?

We gave up trying to get anyone's attention and we just lay there for a little while. We could feel him in there with us, sense his presence in the room. A stillness that filled us up. We didn't even know what time it was because I had made Ty unplug the alarm clock so those little red bars wouldn't keep me up. So I could fall asleep in the total black, clinging to him like we were both falling, and December didn't matter, like it didn't matter if we ever even woke up or not. I couldn't get to my phone, of course, because it was charging in the next room to keep the display from unexpectedly coming to life, swirling all colorful like an oil slick in the street, jarring me awake, and tearing me from my perfect and dreamless sleep. And Ty didn't even have a phone. He said he didn't want one cuz people were always bothering him, but I knew that he just couldn't afford one.

"We can just wait until morning," I said, knowing what he was thinking. "We can just wait until we can see and then we can catch him. Like we did last time."

"Last time was during the day," he said. "It might be 10 PM, for all you know. Do you want to wait seven hours until the sun comes up?"

I could smell the vodka on his breath. It smelled like a headache.

"It might be later. Sunup might only be an hour away," I said, thinking of how much you could see in those post-midnight, pre-sunrise hours when the sky turned grey and somber, like we were looking out from under a tarp stretched out over the whole world.

But I knew we were in a predicament. I knew the snake was extra irritable because we hadn't fed him in a while because we were trying to get caught up on the rent and everything. I knew he would strike the first chance he got, and that he would come looking for warmth in the first place he could find it, which would be in Ty's bed with me and Ty.

"No. We gotta make a move," Ty said. He sounded drunker than he had when we'd gone to bed and I wondered if he had waited for me to fall to sleep so he could slip into the kitchen and have a nip or two.

"Maybe we can throw something and make little Sammy attack," I suggested, calling him little to remind Ty that he was small and fragile and ours.

"And if he bites something then he'll use all his venom on it," Ty said, understanding and co-signing my plan. "Good idea."

"And then we can run for the door."

"No way," and he shifted his body so I couldn't hold onto him anymore, yanking his arm away from me to remind me that it belonged to him. "Then we can attack it."

"No," I said. "Then we can just get out. Then we'll be safe."

"You know what they say in the program," Ty said. I could tell by the sound of the bedsprings squeaking that he was gathering himself into a crouch on the bed in the dark. "God only gives you things you can handle."

That was one of his favorite things to say. He used to say it all the time. I'm not sure he knew what it meant, but I knew just what his face looked like even though I couldn't see it. I thought if I grabbed hold of his arms and held him hard enough he might give up, might decide to stay in bed with me where it was safe and not go out there with Sammy, but I couldn't find him in the dark.

I heard Ty throw the pillow across the room. I heard the pillow thump into the corner and I heard little Sammy fall for it. I was hoping maybe he wouldn't. I was hoping maybe he'd be too smart for it and find a way to crawl up the post of the bed and sneak under the covers with us and bite us both, maybe one fang for each and kill us both dead at exactly the same time. But Sammy didn't do any of that.

We could hear him hissing in the corner, trying to be all tough, warning that pillow not to come closer. The sound of his hiss was like a tiny little puff of air, the sound a Huffy tire makes when you poke it with a blade. The sound was like an admission, a confession; Sssssammy giving in once and for all because once Sammy revealed his position, Ty made a break for the light switch. The lights were so bright when they came on my eyes squeezed shut on their own. I pulled down on my cheeks to spread my eyelids apart, refusing to let my coward eyes snap shut like they wanted to.

I managed to see Ty pick up what was left of the aquarium, a cracked shell collapsing in on itself, and he raised it over his head. He wobbled toward the corner where he'd thrown the pillow, where Sammy had fallen for the trap and he hucked that aquarium, finishing it for good. A fake plastic rock slapped against the wall. The glass splashed across the floor, clacking against the hardwood floor.

Ty picked up the plastic rock and hit Sammy with it. Over and over until the fake rock was coming apart and Sammy had completely stopped moving and just lay there in that way you could tell there was no life left in him. When he was done, Ty held Ssssssammy's body up, its guts blooming from holes Ty had made with the fake rock. He tried not to laugh while he did it, but he couldn't hide it. I could one hundred percent see that he was laughing. It was nice that he tried tho.

"I guess it's male after all," Ty said, inspecting the tail section. "A little boy," he said.

He had gotten his danger for the evening, sure enough.

He tried to comfort me the best way he knew how. He wasn't very good at it. He rubbed my back like he was trying to warm me up and he brought me a box of tissues and then a roll of toilet paper when I used up all the tissues. We checked what time it was and it turned out to be around 1:30 AM, which was about what I had figured, but there was no way we could have confirmed that with the room as dark as I had wanted it, so dark Ty couldn't even see that cheapo watch of his. I cried until my head felt all blown up and swollen, like someone put an airhose into my brain. I cried harder than I had last December.

I fell asleep holding onto Ty, but only because he was the only one there. If it was The Brighton Beach Murderer, a Catholic Priest, or Dad I would have hung onto them just as tite. But I didn't feel like we were falling anymore, clinging to each other as we plummeted arm and arm to our deaths. The lights coming on cured me of all that. I could see things for what they were. And accept them too.

So I told my little snake story at my next AA meeting. I kept my eye on the clock, trying not to talk for longer than five minutes. My sponsor told me no one wants to hear you talk for more than five minutes. I told them all about the snake and the lights and how Ty killed poor little Sssssssammy. And that was it. I just said my piece and said that I would keep coming back and then someone else started their share. No one clapped for me or anything. That doesn't usually happen at meetings like they show on TV. Unless there is a guest speaker. And even then sometimes people don't clap.

And that's it. Now you can see. Now you know that it was Ty's fault, but partly my fault too. And now you see that it's not that old saw about the talking snake. Who even could believe a story about a talking snake anyways? What is this, The freaking Bible? Anyway, now you can probably easily see what I was hoping you would take away from all this. Can't you?

THE STEP-BY-STEP GUIDE TO HOME EXORCISM

She called the number when nothing else worked. She didn't think anyone would answer. She'd left Carter in their room, making a constrictor of the sweat-soaked sheets, little vials of holy water lined up along the bedside table like still-open browser tabs, waiting to be useful again.

The phone rang past the point when it should have gone to voicemail. It rang past the point someone would have ignored it. It rang in such a way—those bells manic, tidy, and near—that she could tell she was calling a landline. The sound of the phone ringing in her ear was the trilling of a great mechanical bird, the intervals of its warbles woeful and lonely, reaching out to some distant space where the magic needed to retrieve Carter was real. Where such things as demon possession and exorcisms were common. Accepted. Some dimension halfway between a television show and the myth we have of the past—where help from priests and family members is so common that they swarm the possessed body like white blood cells, colluding to uninfect the infected.

While the phone rang, she held the book—as if the

connection could not be made without the book acting as a totem.

The book had come in the mail one day, she was pretty sure. Roz had not remembered ordering it, but she had ordered so many things. Crosses to hang on the wall and around her neck, industrial-grade rubber gloves, the holy water vials, plastic sheeting, blessed palms, safety restraints, five-gallon buckets, bolt locks for the bedroom door, cleaning products, incense, glass, and calk to replace the broken window he smashed with his head, sutures, bandages, gauze, and extra-strength Excedrin by the case for the daily misery of her stress-induced migraines. The packages showed up like they had volition of their own, schedules and agendas they had to keep.

Carter had been like this for months. In the beginning, she thought it would go away, she thought she could beat it back with will and devotion, but she'd had to take vacation days and sick time from work and then FMLA time, and still the evil squirmed inside him. Little cutworms in the corn.

He hadn't worked the entire year leading up to his possession. He'd subjected Roz to the chaos of his whims, sometimes showing up with stacks of money he'd spend on her, taking her downtown or buying her new dresses and tall boots, and other times she'd find him stealing her cash, her credit cards, jewelry he'd bought for her. She watched him do it like a novice watches a chess master execute the maneuvers with native aplomb and thoughtless effortlessness.

In April it got really bad. That's when things became physical. By May he couldn't leave the room, couldn't even leave the bed, and she had to bring him food and change his messy sheets every day. Forgetting other activities in favor of loads of laundry and rubbing ointment on bedsores. It got to the point where one day oozed into the next, where things appeared to be coming apart, and she became desperate for some kind of relief. That's when she called the number.

The phone continued to ring, and Roz sat in the office where they put the workout equipment. She had no intention of hanging up, the ringing a respite from the growling, the clawing, the spitting, the screaming that Carter was doing in the bedroom.

She'd been sleeping downstairs in the den. She didn't realize until it was too late that she should have put him in the office with the workout equipment so she could sleep in her own bed. She wasn't sure it would have done her any good anyway. She did not sleep anymore. Sometimes she doubted that she ever had, the practice of hallucinating in a comatose state seeming so ill-advised and peculiar to her once she no longer did it.

She let the phone ring as a lullaby for her ear, the tone a cathode-tube television stuck between stations. She was surprised when the person on the other end finally answered. The phone must have rung a hundred times. When the woman answered, she seemed annoyed that Roz had let the phone ring so many times.

"I didn't think anyone was going to answer," Roz said.

"What do you want?" Roz heard the voice on the other end of the phone say.

"I think I have something of yours," Roz said. "I think I have your book."

"Which book?" the woman wanted to know.

The Book

The book was hardly a book. It was a three-ring binder with photocopied pages, some in translucent sleeves, some stapled together, some folded into the pockets of the binder. One of the sheets said, "The Step by Step Guide to Home Exorcism," so that is what Roz had begun calling it in her mind. She had a hard time organizing the resources. They were hardly coherent, and yet a narrative emerged.

There were section tabs dedicated to Theft, Lying, Perversion, Mendaciousness.

> The demon controls the host and the demons are nasty creatures. Mewing, screaming, animalistic creatures. They emerge when a secular subject matter is introduced. Foul language, sexual excess and perversion will always interest them. But they are very clever. They know how to evade detection and often mask their presence by imitating some other malady: drug addiction, female hysteria, drapetomania, leprosy, imbecilic lunacy, or other moral insanities . . .

The book made demands, offered comfort, was sometimes surly, the way a parent might be. The way a lover might be. Roz was having trouble navigating her relationship with the book, and when she found the number, she knew she was going to have to call it.

The Woman on the Phone

By the sound of her voice, Roz guessed the woman on the phone was younger than she. The liquid of her vocal cords, still new, just out of the package, like everything else young people took for granted. But there was a heavy that burdened the young woman. A knowing.

"Your number was in the book," Roz explained.

"How did you get the book?" the girl on the other end of the phone demanded. "How did it come to you?"

Roz knew she couldn't answer the question. She wondered if Carter had bought it as a laugh or as some desperate attempt to save himself before he was too far gone to leave the house. She'd found it when she'd cleared off the bookshelves in their bedroom and dumped the books in the kitchen to keep him from vomiting on them. When she returned to the room, the shelves were gaping and bare in their room like they'd been robbed, empty except for that book.

"There is a note in it. To someone named Volina. It says to 'use the book as an offense against evil.' Are you Volina? Do you know her?"

"Are you telling me that you don't even know where you got it from?"

"He's not getting any better," Roz said. "That's the only reason I called."

Neither woman spoke for a long time, the line falling as silent as the hush that follows the slamming of a door. Roz could tell what the woman on the other end of the line was thinking. Roz tried to remember if telepathy was a possible side effect of demon possession.

"It takes a while," the younger woman said, finally admitting that she knew the book to which Roz was referring.

"You've done it before?"

"You have to try to make a routine of it. Do the same thing every day. That's the only way you'll be able to keep it up for long enough."

"Did you make this book?" Roz asked.

"But you should probably just leave."

"I'm not going to leave. He's my husband."

"You should probably just burn the place to the ground and move to Alaska or somewhere like that."

Roz wanted to hang up on the little shit, this girl—because that's what she sounded like, like a girl. Not like a woman. Even though she had a landline like someone trapped in the twentieth century, and she had all this knowledge and experience, she talked like a girl. But Roz knew she couldn't hang up. More than any other time in her entire life, she felt beholden to someone. Roz knew she would obey any command this girl proffered. She was just grateful the girl seemed to be giving her the option between saving Carter and burning the place down. Roz knew deep down that if this little girl told her she had to hit the place with a wrecking ball, that it was the only option, she would do it. She would listen. She would obey.

"I want to save him," Roz said. "I have to try."

Even that felt like an admission that she might not be able to do it. Even that made it seem like it was over.

"He doesn't have anyone else? A brother? A girlfriend?"

"I told you, we're married."

"Yeah. Well, you are gonna need some help, so it would actually be easier if he was cheating on you."

"He had a sponsor," Roz admitted. "But he hasn't been to a meeting in a while."

"You better call the sponsor."

Don D.

Don D., as he always introduced himself, arrived that night. He brought with him a pizza and a carton of cigarettes.

"I'm not hungry and I don't smoke," Roz tried to tell him.

"How long has this been going on?"

"Which part?"

"You better eat something."

So they did. They finished the pizza and a pack of cigarettes, and they barely talked. Roz didn't know what to say to someone in the program, and he didn't know what to say to a woman whose husband was possessed by demonic forces.

"Do you want to see him?" she finally asked.

When You Will Finally Heal

> You will come to this method when other methods have failed completely. The body of the possessed is quite as abnormal as his mind. Those out of control, maladjusted to life, in full flight from reality, or mentally defective.
>
> The befogged at the gates of death.
>
> Frothy emotional appeals will be met with ridicule and sometimes violence. Only the reliance upon a higher power can allow a possessed person the ability to remake their life.

Praxis

Carter had stopped throwing up in the toilet and had started just throwing up on himself, all over the bed. He pissed and shat himself too, and he would try to grab Roz while she cleaned him. She'd run the hose in from the garden and soak him down, then cover him in towels and blankets. He'd snarl. He told Don that his wife had fucked up teeth and that his kids would probably never talk to him again. Don told Carter that the first step was to admit that he had a problem.

Once the initial wave of insults were done, they all got

to work, reading the book, doing what it said, following a daily routine.

Four weeks in and the woman on the other end of the phone started calling Roz. Roz would answer it exhausted, wearing rubber gloves.

"How is it going?"

"Not great. I got fired from my job."

"This is like your dream come true. You've always wanted someone to save and now you really have one."

"You're not as smart as you think you are."

"Neither are you."

Identifying a Demonic Presence

> It is not difficult to identify a demonic presence in a person. The host's behavior becomes subhuman and animalistic. It is not uncommon for a host to develop a stare. A way of looking when they think they are not being observed. A longing inherent in the way their eyes reach out for the dawn.
>
> Godlessness, perversion, and carnality are typical preoccupations of the host of a demon presence.

Reading Comprehension

"How long have you had this book?" Don asked her after Carter was done swearing at them, putting cigarettes out on his arm, and throwing feces.

"I'm not sure. I think it was in a box of books my mom was getting rid of."

"It's weird."

"That I don't know where I got it, or the book itself is weird."

"This whole thing is a puzzle," he said, staring down

at the scattered documents.

Don pulled out a sheet of paper with a set of instructions. There were hand-drawn sketches showing how to hold the subject down when you prayed over them.

"I can't make heads or tails of the book," she admitted. "I try to read it, but it just doesn't make any sense. It's like lorem ipsum text."

"That's how I felt the first time I tried to read the big book," Don said.

"Alcoholics always think everyone else is an alcoholic."

"I'm just saying the words maybe haven't revealed themselves to you yet."

"It says we have to read the Bible to him," she said, pointing to the passage in front of him.

"Do you have one?" he asked.

"I have a couple, but I don't know which one to pick."

They read from the Children's Bible because it skipped all the begats and the dietary restrictions, and because they liked the pictures. Carter didn't seem to listen when they read. He just tried to stick things up himself and down his throat and smashed empty glass bottles against the wall.

Ways to Recognize Demonic Influence

- Anger. They can respond violently to the slightest oppression, frustration, or loss. Without grace or moderation.
- There is a perversion in the lives of the possessed. They cannot control their vulgar desires and their crass requests for such. They are willing and capable of using foul language in pursuit, during, and in reference to sexual escapades. They eschew monogamy, often militating against such concepts.

- The demon thrives in an environment where the host is mentally, physically, or spiritually weak.
- The demon will encourage its host to indict and denunciate.
- They traffic in untruth, often using a lie when the truth would suffice. You will see in the possessed the deceiver's delight. The smile of the successfully elusive.

The Dog in the Meadow

She walked along the bike trail near her home. She hadn't left the house for weeks before Don had shown up. With him watching over Carter, she could shower, dress in her long tweed coat and scarf, and walk out along the path behind their home, looking at the Halloween decorations—the kids too fast on their bikes, the leaves mostly fallen.

The world had moved on without her, and she could see no one concerned with Carter or his possession. The dads on their lawns raking leaves suspicious; someone old on their porch holding what looked like rubber tubing; teenagers at the skate park wrapping themselves around each other, violence on their hips. They all watched her until she passed.

Up ahead in the meadow she could see a dog wrestling with something. It shook whatever it had its teeth sunk into. As she got closer she could tell it was a heron, or some great bird like that. She ran at the dog, screaming at it, waving her arms. By the time she got to it the heron stood over the carcass of the dog, its wings spread, its beak proud. It seemed to be looking at her, daring her to confront it. She listened for the dog's crying but there was none.

Roz and Don

"Sometimes I wonder if this is really him," she said to Don after they'd weathered another day full of insults and violence. "If there is no demon and this is just how he is. Mean. Cruel."

"Everyone can be mean and cruel," Don told her. He stared at her, his eyes unblinking, intense.

"Sometimes I resent that I'm the one who has to save him."

"He's just sick, Roz," Don said. He sipped tea she had made for him. It was too hot, but he sipped it anyway. Roz looked at him, his shoulders heaped upon his back and arms, his flesh thick like a hide. He seemed so much denser than Carter. So much sturdier. He was slower, too. Older. Stiffer. He groaned when he stood up from a chair, but he did so with a weary dignity that Roz liked. She wanted to ask him about his sobriety, how that had come to be, but she felt like maybe she shouldn't.

Sometimes Don hovered inches above the floor, wobbling the way two magnets with the same polarity used to do in tenth-grade science class. Like he was balancing himself on a ball, like some clown or seal. But there was no ball and no magnets.

"Is that what they teach you to do in AA?"

"I thought everyone could do this."

"You're either the best person to help me with this or the worst."

Matthew 24:15:

> So when you are standing in the holy place and you see the abomination that causes desolation, let the reader understand.

Ecclesiology

When Roz called the number again the girl on the other end knew what Roz was going to say. That she and Don had spent weeks following the instructions of the book. That they had tried to adhere to it to the letter. That they had worked together and beat back feelings of affection for one another because it seemed like having and entertaining those emotions was somehow disrespectful to Carter and not in the spirit of the thing. They turned their affections off and let the book guide them.

"We did all that for him, for Carter, and then he left," Roz said.

"I know," the girl said. And for a moment, Roz thought it was because Carter was with her. That he was in her tiny apartment, as Roz imagined it, with her old rotary phone and a beat-up kitchen with scarred tiles, and he was in her rickety old bed, not spitting or pissing or vomiting on it, but waiting for her to return so he could make love to her. But Roz knew that wasn't true. The girl knew because it had happened to her. The demon possession, the selflessness of the recovery process, the pain of facing that once it was over, only ruined things were left in its absence.

"I was married when it happened," the girl explained, sounding more and more like a woman, her words more and more matching that laugh she had. "After the exorcism was over, we tried to do new things. We tried to go to horse races. That was weird. Neither of us even liked animals or had ever been gambling, but we thought that somehow, we might all of a sudden start going together. Sometimes I think if I hadn't chased off that demon, we woulda been together forever. "

"Once the possession was over, it was like there was

nothing left to do. "

"Now you get it."

"It was like once I'd seen him like that . . . "

"Yup."

Neither of them had to speak once Roz got to that realization. They just sat with the reality of it, each knowing one another's grief.

"I'm not sure I even miss him," Roz finally said to break the silence.

"Yeah," said the girl, sounding like a girl again. "That's the worst part."

Coffee Shop

Roz ran into Don once more. At a coffee shop where he sat sipping tea, his hands shaking. He was slumped into one of the iron-wrought chairs, and it trembled beneath him like a loose shingle. The coffee shop used to be a mom-and-pop hardware, and the old store haunted the space: the tables occupying the space where the plumbing fixtures used to be, the espresso machine taking the place of the hammers. It didn't feel like a coffee shop, though every symbol in the space signified its intention to be a coffee shop, with its hissing steam, its faux-vintage lighting fixtures, and the smell of mocha. Before she ran into Don there, it had been Roz's favorite coffee shop. She tried to remember if she'd told him about it.

"You probably heard I relapsed," he said.

"Who would I hear that from?"

"I'm gonna start back up going to meetings this week," he said, assuring her though she hadn't asked.

"Have you seen Carter?" she wanted to know.

"He's doing great. Did 90 meetings in 90 days, got a

new sponsor, started chairing meetings. He's doing great."

"That's good," Roz said, though she wasn't sure she meant it. She wasn't sure what she wanted to hear.

"Do you want to sit?" he asked, starting to stand, like a Carhartt-wearing prince.

"No," she said, her coffee steaming in her hands, burning the tips of her fingers. "I gotta get going."

"Yeah," he said, slumping back down into his chair. Accepting that his chance for that kind of thing to happen was gone.

"If you see him, would you tell him to stop calling me?" she said.

"He was calling you?" Don asked, snapped from his sullenness by this new riddle. "When was he calling you?"

"I've been getting calls from an unknown number. I thought . . . "

"Maybe," he said, squinting and shrugging and shaking his head. "Could be him."

"He's with someone else," Roz said, realizing that as a possibility for the first time.

"You're not supposed to date people from the program, but everyone usually does."

She told him that it had been good to see him, that he looked good, even though she hated seeing him and he looked like a bright rubber ball deflated, and she vowed to never go back to that coffee shop again.

Epilogue

Roz lay in her bed, the stripped mattress still sweat-stained from Carter's efforts with the demon. The exorcism finished, the demon scissored from him and set loose, she traced his name into the page of a book with her index, hoping to coax him back. She stared up at the ceiling as the sunset changed its color, and she tried to ignore the ringing of the cellphone. It had been ringing for what seemed like hours, and no button she pressed, no setting designed to send a caller to voicemail, not flushing the phone down the toilet, nor hitting it with a wrench, could get it to stop. She knew the person on the other end would not relent. She knew she'd have to answer it eventually.

SUNSHOWERS

We are spending the week at a faux-functional horse-riding and fishing destination for those denizens of cities who don't know any better. The place is a performance. A bit of theater meant to convince people with soft hands and internet addictions that somewhere buried deep inside them—where they keep the knowledge of their common ancestry with bonobos—they are rugged and of a piece with the natural world. The ranch flatters. It tells its visitants that they are who they think they are; they are who they mean to be. America is filled with such spots, places that were once operational but are now, working exclusively on the gasoline of nostalgia, serving only to perpetuate an idea.

The staff at the ranch look at the guests with the dim glow of recognition, the wattage from their smiles meant to stall while they grapple for a name. They lead the horses with leather straps, toss bags of feed into the backs of swollen pickup trucks, and walk with a purpose that is self-aware, histrionic, and practiced.

I've been invited to this place despite my job, despite our looming money problems.

My dinner companions—my wife, brother-in-law, their mother who has orchestrated this retreat, and other assorted family—have decided to dine on the patio every night, overlooking the mountains. I prefer the creaky interior of the dining room to the soggy patio under an always rain-soaked awning, but they have decreed the patio to be preferable, and I am in no position to negotiate. Despite my distaste for the location, I am always the first one to arrive. They make me wait. They do this on purpose because I am not one of them, and they look down on me. They would never say this, of course, but it has never been difficult for me to know what opinions a person thinks they are holding close to their breast.

They have their own rhythms, probably established through habits that are remote to me—fundraisers, foundations, airport lounges, evenings out—and I am always just a step too slow to catch the door, just a bit too late to hear the whole of a conversation. Under normal circumstances, I would text or call my fellow diners upon arrival, but none of our phones work in the Adirondacks. Even the clocks are somehow wrong, and after a few hours we all begin leaving the phones in our rooms, not even plugged in as the full battery would just remind us of all the things our devices no longer do. None of us are used to the sovereignty. We luxuriate in it as if it were a bubble bath. As we wander around the grounds of the mountain resort in a lather, we run into one another, stunned but acting pleased to be in each other's company.

⌘ i introduce her

I see the girl before I meet her. She is at the bar reading off a list of drinks for a table to which she is attending.

She acts oblivious to how much of the room the shard of her frame attracts.

The bartender, short and thick as a callus, has his own agenda; "I don't believe that for a second," he tells her, ignoring her drink order. "Every seventeen-year-old here says she's got a boyfriend, but they never do."

The bartender's smile is a crooked river swollen by the rain. He is angling, but the girl knows how to position herself with a smile, a word, a gesture. She pushes off the bar like she is shoving off the side of a pool into the deep end. She leaves with a wave.

The bartender is sure to make some young girl's life miserable with an unwanted pregnancy or a too-quick ascent into the stratospheres of adulthood, but this one, the seventeen-year-old with the alleged beau, isn't to be the victim. He isn't really the one I am worried about anyway.

The real problems are the ones who don't talk about it. The ones who aren't comfortable revealing their lustful hearts in public. The ones so buried under shame that they would never be anything but polite with those for whom they long. The real ogres are the ones who are complete gentlemen.

I talk to the girl for the first time on the patio, on the first night. It is right after I meet Clark, who is the one who introduces me to her.

As I wait on the patio and I stare out over the mountains, I think about my wife and son. I wonder what would happen were one of us to slip down the side of the mountain or be mauled to death by a bobcat. I think about what might become of our triumvirate were one of the three of us to be disappeared. My wife and son bereft but strong; my wife and I suicidal and estranged; my son and I lost.

While I think these thoughts, I feel Clark's too-familiar hand on my shoulder. Clark's job seems strangely amorphous, and his position strikes me as mainly ceremonial; an honorary member of the management team with no ostensible power and yet tremendous influence. He smiles at me, his face cracked at the eyes by the sun and filled with a tender grit. He is always accompanied by a cologne of bug spray and sweat. His hat slips down his forehead and covers his eyes.

"I haven't seen you do very much," he tells me, his voice loud and unregulated. His eyes pore over my fleshy body, and he evaluates and categorizes me as if I were a potential hire, lying on my resume. He is ruddy and all capable sinew, despite his clearly advanced age.

"Haven't had much time," I tell him, beginning to see how this might go. We've been led around from the moment we spilled from the black car. The staff surrounded us when we arrived, unencumbering us so we could infest. A woman who looked like a librarian advertised all the myriad activities to us: fly-fishing lessons in Lake George, photography hikes up Mount Marcy, horse-riding lessons at the ranch. Each excursion described seemed more idyllic than the previous, and each one seemed less and less appealing. My conversation with Clark makes it clear that we have been monitored during this orientation, our capabilities measured, our proclivities assumed.

"Make sure you get signed up for the whitewater rafting," Clark sings.

"Of course I will," I say.

I sit through his line of questioning as my eyes dart around, looking for my belated party.

"We must have the same barber," he says, lifting his hat and running his hand over the stubble of his shaved skull and then pointing at my own mostly hairless pate. He says it in a practiced way that makes me wonder if he always finds the baldest guy at the resort to harass. I wait politely and try to smile as he runs through a string of bald jokes meant to link us.

The young waitress whom the bartender was flirting with has begun slipping around and in between us, setting up the ten-top that will be our table.

"And I assume you've met Emily," he says and holds his hand out like he is ushering me into his car or his living room. "Or as I call her, 'Boom Boom.'"

He smiles and gives me a crass, full-bodied wink.

"She needed a nickname, and the first day she walked in, I just thought it fit . . . " he pauses for effect and elbows me in the ribs as he adds the punchline, " . . . for some reason."

I look to see if she has heard him.

"I kinda like it," Emily says to me and him both as she glides past us, holding a tray full of drinks, the beverages scheduled for a table made up of well-groomed frowns.

"She reminds me of a girl I met when I was in the service," Clark says as we watch her try to match each diner with their alcohol.

I wonder where he was stationed, but I can't bring myself to ask for fear of giving him reason to boast, for fear that he has a great war to tell me he helped to win. I make the assumption that he spent his twenties stationed in Europe but without seeing combat, spending his time instead falling in love with some burlesque dancer who broke his heart and for whom he has searched for ever after—sifting through each successive generation like a panner slipping his hands through the sand, hoping to find gold.

At dinner, Emily buzzes from one table to another, forgetting to bring bread or appropriate silverware, screwing up orders and spilling water on guests. All of her foibles are excused, however. The thought that she might be scolded or held accountable seems never to occur to her. She is a hummingbird, fleeting and random, visiting and then disappearing in the same breath.

⌘ what she looks like to me

The next morning, I watch her as she serves us breakfast. Emily puts old slang into use—saying the hungover patrons have a "case of the zings," and calling all compliments "horsefeathers"—employing the out-of-fashion phrases like she has only just learned them. And perhaps she has. Her clothes drape off her. Like a flag lazing in the still heat. She is related to farmers. She believes that despite the negativity Monsanto receives in the press, they are necessary, and she doesn't think about it any further than that. It is enough for her to know that uncles and cousins rely on the company and its products.

When she leaves, the coffee pot perilous in her hand, she doesn't turn, she twirls.

Slender and egret-like, Emily wears a dress that is low cut in the front with a mere few strings in the back. Her tattoos are small and plentiful and are lined up like bread crumb trails that lead to the even more sensual parts of her. Lines cut across her bicep and thigh, seeming to bi-

and tri-furcate her body into pieces like a butcher's chart advertising the cuts of meat available to customers. I cultivate an image of Clark being the one to ink her. She knows why she was hired.

Despite her beauty, they work her hard. I know just how her skin cracks from the dishwashing fluid, how her hands itch from the chemicals, how the pinks swollen across the backs of her hands are loud and ugly. I know that one irritated spot vibrating and elusive, deep within the palm, refusing to be found, daring to be scratched. I know just how her left side aches from shouldering drinks, how she tries to work the knots out of her shoulder every night.

⌘ i introduce the man and his wife

Emily is unlike the women I usually fall for. Were she my type, I would have been just as helpless as the married man at the other table. The man is tall, with curly hair, Caucasian in that quintessential way where his facial growth accents his features, his apathy and laziness somehow benefiting him, making him more attractive. Even his leisure clothes are expensive. The man is surrounded by people who obsessively follow sports, desperate to be "in the know," to have something to discuss in great detail that is not themselves. His eyes stare out from under a meticulously tattered baseball cap which somehow doesn't clash or invalidate the effect of his expensive shorts, fleece, and trendy sandals. He is complete, and the world belongs to him. I can tell just by looking at him. Just by the way he looks at the waitress, by the way he refrains from staring down her shirt when she bends over to take the menus from him and from his wife and child. I can see him congratulating himself on a job well done.

Such restraint, he must be telling himself. Such chivalry. To allow her some shred of privacy. Though he wants her, of course. Every pierced part of her. The tongue with its stud gleaming like the last light left on in an otherwise abandoned dormitory; the innermost cartilage fold of her left ear bangled with a ring, her body veneered with expensive tattoos and cheap jewelry; her voice strained by cigarette and marijuana smoke; her long blond hair that reaches the middle of her back even when it is flipped backwards off the top of her head like some great lion's mane; even the bad breath, the acne, the poor grammar.

⌘ i describe the horse corral

The women who work at the horse corral are wide, dark, and Rubenesque, their bottoms snug against the denim that they wear. They hoist saddles onto horses with sounds women usually keep out of reach but for their lovers. I am told there are no male ranch hands anymore, the jobs going to these capable women instead.

They are gruff but also beautiful. Little bits of perspiration accumulate on their upper lips. They move with vigor and purpose. They are poorly drawn tableaux walked straight off of murals and into the dust. Despite the heat, their flannel shirts are buttoned to the top button, defiant and almost delusional. They live in tiny bullet-shaped trailers, stowed behind the corral like unpaired shoes tossed into a closet and on top of one another. I wonder how many ranch hands occupy each dwelling.

The horses are mostly old, overweight, and discarded from other ranches, but they are still majestic. Their lethargy reads as dignity, and they snort at the children who are perched on their backs for photos. The horses taking the food offered them like a wronged lover accepting the money she is owed. The dull sound of hooves on the thick dirt is strangely tantalizing in its repetition and its timbre. I have the distinct feeling that I want the popping sound of trotting on the inside of my mouth.

"They are impressive," I say to one of the ranch hands as my child is led around on the back of a horse with a face that looks sour and reluctant. I choose my words carefully. "They are like machines come to life."

She does not react. It is as if she does not speak the same language as me and for a moment I wonder if she does.

"Would you like to take a picture," she asks finally, as if there is nothing else that might occur to her to say.

⌘ what emily sounds like to me

"I appreciate you," Emily says to everyone when she walks away, as if she looks forward to returning.

"Much obliged," he says archly, anachronistically, and not meaning it.

She does not know how people talk, I realize. She has not met enough of them. She has always retreated to the outdoors because there are still places where there is no entry fee, where the wild undulates beneath one's feet and doesn't ask a tax. When she is brought to the movie theater, a diner, or even the mall, I realize, she feels like there is a clock ticking down to the moment her poverty will be discovered. She has always preferred to be alone and outdoors where it is safe, where she cannot be bothered.

I get lunch alone, separated from my travel companions. They don't know that I have arrived in the dining hall and that I watch them from across the room as they whisper to one another.

⌘ i describe the man's wife

The man's wife orders the staff around like she has never been obedient, like she began her life telling people to serve and has never considered acting any other way. She hands her children to childcare workers who possess an expertise most reserve for athletics and card tricks.

The man earned her the same way he earned everything else in his life, his career and achievements and possessions, by being proud and comfortable with his position in the world. He earned her, perfect once, when she was young and without flaws, by buying in totally, by synthesizing his inner life with the world at large until there was no difference between what it could give him and what he wanted from it.

⌘ what emily wants

She has applied to school, I hear her tell people. She has even applied to a few out-of-state places too, she insists, as if that makes it more valid. She says it to distinguish herself from peers of hers who have also dropped out of high school and who have also not yet gotten their GEDs, and who also work in similarly tourist-supported places, serving fulfillment of one kind or another to out-of-towners.

Even as she describes her future plans though, to

supervisors, to guests, to co-workers, she gets the feeling that she is being pitied. It is the same feeling she had when she was a child and, after wowing a grandparent with her knowledge of the word "hieroglyphics," tried to impress other adults, only to realize that they were not amazed, but merely charmed.

She has not applied to school, of course. She wouldn't know where to start. She expects that one day college will come find her, the opportunity unfurling itself before her like the red carpets on the television shows she likes to watch. In the meantime, she thinks about what she might study and decides Biology since she is pretty much a nature trail guide already, as she often has to explain to the guests what indigenous bugs and plants are beautiful but poisonous and which ones are merely beautiful.

⌘ sex

Emily brings with her a repertoire gained under the stars and in backseats with boys, barely old enough to drive, a repertoire acquired by acting impish and pretending, often, to be confused. I know just what kind of cheap, oil-stinking cars those boys drove, with fast food crushed into the seats and exhaust systems rattling beneath. Cars with dashboards lit up with little red and yellow icons that the drivers could never raise the money to address and so are ignored.

She is far from competent, the man is almost delighted to note, but she is adequate. Her lovemaking is raw and honest in a way that the man's wife's is not. At the beginning, perhaps it was like that. The man cannot quite remember. Anymore his wife must be asphyxiated, choked, dominated in a way that concentrates the euphoria of intercourse. At first it was a thrill for him too, but the routine has somehow made it feel contrived and boring. With the girl it is not like that. It is honest and feral. He can smell her rancid breath and her unwashed privates and armpits. It does not occur to her to try to mask these things.

In the pool shed, past dark and among the chemicals and plastic tools, they reveal themselves to each other. They present what they want, what they have developed with other people, what they have inherited, and what they haven't shared with another soul. They are like two musicians meeting and letting their instruments speak for them. He smiles and inhales, kissing her warm and sunburnt skin. She admits him, relishing the letting.

⌘ will you remember me?

At dinner, she recites the specials. She is aloof, polite, formal. She is kind to the man's wife and child but not too kind. She asks about their food but is curt when his wife asks her to take the food back, just like she would were she not sleeping with the woman's husband. As I watch her maneuver the husband, wife, and their toddler-aged daughter, I realize that she has done this before. She is the expert, not him.

"Will you remember me in five years?" he asks her the next time they are alone.

"Will you remember me next week?" she asks.

"We might be back next year."

"Maybe by then you'll be single," Emily says.

"Who knows," he says, gruff, annoyed.

They are beyond being the free agents of love, each of their little grooming rituals now already taken for granted by the other, he grateful for the way she applies mascara, she charmed by the smell of his pungent, expensive cologne.

He doesn't acknowledge her when he and his wife pass her on the way to drop their daughter off at the resort daycare. They continue silently along the dirt path to the cabin where teen girl caretakers lead the children in rituals of abandonment. They craft birdfeeders and paint rocks. The children do not long for their parents but instead focus on the tasks before them like they are little leatherworkers and machinists, as if their menial jobs will conjure their parents if done correctly.

The man's wife reaches her hands out, full of red-headed baby, and indicates her exit by announcing, "We'll be back when you close." The man's wife is twisted and sour, like once-bright fruit left in the sun. She has the look of a person who feels she has been swindled. I can tell. This vacation has been long-earned. And the man complies, leaving the child without so much as a word. Gushing over the girl, as he normally would, might make his wife feel jealous or guilty. He turns away from the child, whom he adores. He walks away and tries to ignore her wailing.

⌘ again at dinner

The patio is closed off because a large group has reserved it, though when I walk past, it seems they occupy only a quarter of it. My travel companions and I are in the dining room like I originally suggested, but I am not happy about it. I feel guilty about getting what I want, guilty that the food I cannot afford is being paid for by a patron, and that my desire for where to sit is being satisfied.

I see the woman who cleans our room emptying a

bucket into a utility sink. She makes me uncomfortable; her thick wrists and skin the color of my wife's too-sweet coffee. Emily is not there and neither are the man and his wife. I imagine them off somewhere enjoying themselves, Emily occupying the role of big sister to the young child, their faces all a warped smear of joy. I know this can never be the case.

I am asked about the duck for a second time. I nod, hoping it is the correct answer. I can see recognition in the face of our waiter, a thin young man with dirt around his fingernails, with a small stain just above the belt line of his white, button-down shirt. I hate him.

My travel companions ask me when school will begin again, if I ever keep in touch with my students, what I think about recent legislation regarding curriculum. My conversation acquits itself, I think, and soon they go back to speaking with each other about what really interests them, what they really want to talk about.

⌘ the wife goes into town

"I think I might go to town to shop," the man's wife says the next morning.

The man cannot believe his luck, but he knows he cannot reveal his joy.

The man's wife has met several other women, one of whom is from near where they live. The women agree to engage in the pantomime that this coincidence is a miracle, as if pockets of affluence and opportunity are not clustered and concentrated. As if finding people from your income group at a place only accessible to your income group is something plump with meaning, something suggesting destiny. The women feel like they should become friends. All their smiles are twisted at the end in the same way and pointed at one another in some polite form of a standoff, their weapons beautiful but no less deadly than those of a cowboy in an old film. Mutually assured destruction lurks in their laughs. The women lob pithy remarks at one another, each compliment a threat dressed in couture fashion. They all lay hands on one another in acts that approximate empathy but are too frigid and practiced to be the real thing.

"How much will you spend?" he asks.

"Don't be like that," the man's wife says and scowls. "We are supposed to be on vacation. It's not like you didn't buy those golf clubs we had to lug through the airport."

Though he knew he was getting what he wanted, he was disappointed that his wife was not more suspicious of his play. There was no semblance of the woman he had met when they were young, the jealous one who threatened his ex, the devoted one who nursed him back to health from hangovers even on occasions when he had been the only one drinking.

The man and the girl spend all day together, trying to avoid other people and then trying to ascertain whether or not anyone knows their secret. In the man's cabin they make love, but the man is disappointed that the cabin seems to belong to her. He wants her for himself, on his own territory, among his expensive things and his stack of books—worn copies of books he wants people to know he has read, books by Stephen Pinker, Howard Bloom, and James Salter. But the girl is so familiar with the cabin that she adjusts the windows herself, doesn't fumble with blinds like he does, and leaps into bed with a squeal as if they are pretending to be in her home and not his.

The old springs of the bed groan beneath them like fresh snow being crushed underfoot for the first time.

⌘ rain

It is raining when they leave the room, but the sun is out. They don't talk about it. He looks up at the sky, the sun a piece of licked candy stuck to the construction paper blue. He wrinkles his face against the raindrops, and Emily runs toward the dining cabin to start her shift. She squeals and holds her hands above her head uselessly, fingers akimbo. Her jean shorts are too big, they are baggy and vaguely masculine. Her legs look like strands dangling beneath her. Her shirt is tight and white. She is happy.

⌘ endings

By the end of the week, it seems the secret is out. The man's wife lounges in the hot tub while the man and the girl walk with one another near the lake. She has gotten time away from her duties to talk to him.

"Did you say you would or wouldn't remember me?" she asks him.

Later, as the man packs up the car to leave, the wife strokes the girl's hair and coos. She is grateful the man has had this distraction.

As they pull away in their late model luxury car, the engine barely a whisper against the creaking sound of cicadas, I sit in the dining room, again waiting for my companions. My brother-in-law has mentioned, feverishly, conspiratorially, that he has slept with one of the women on the staff, and I wonder which one. I wonder if it is the woman who cleans our room or someone from the daycare. I wonder if the girl I have slept with will remember me. I wonder if we will be back.

Clark and the bartender sit at the bar while Emily makes her own drinks. They tease her, trying to guess her weight, overestimating dramatically. They fail to get a reaction from her.

I drink flat club soda and stare at her reflection in the mirror behind the bar as she places her drinks on a tray and holds a smirk up between her and the two men. She twirls away with a tray of drinks that I am sure are all wrong.

"Could I get another one of these?" I ask her as she walks past.

"You bet," she says, placing a vodka tonic down before me.

I count the singles I have in my wallet, wondering how the man made his first entreaty, wondering how it all worked.

"Are you a guest?" she wonders.

"Not for long," I tell her, tucking the few bills I have back into my pocket.

"Well, ta ta," she says and spins back toward the kitchen, buoyed by the sweet smell of her shampoo and lit by the warm glow of her smile.

IN RESPONSE TO YOUR E-NEWSLETTER RE: PETER GABRIEL'S UPCOMING SUMMER TOUR DATES

To Whom It May Concern:

This isn't going to be one of those long emails. Not like the others. I am only going to say enough so that it will be perfectly clear to whomsoever is reading this, that I do not want to be subscribed to your email service/newsletter any longer nor in any capacity. Your constant and insistent invitations for me to click on your links and purchase your products are met with, on my end, nothing but frustration. For some reason, despite my initial, measured requests to be removed and my later, more vehement protestations, your emails continue to arrive in my inbox. No matter what I do, no matter what button I press, no matter to whom I address my emails, I continue receiving these unwanted communiqués.

I have tried to respond to the emails that show up in my inbox, but that only gets me an automated response that says, "The email address you have reached is not monitored." When I have tried clicking on the "unsubscribe" button, which is all the way at the bottom of the email and in a font so small it can barely be found, that link just brings me to a website form that asks for my email address. Upon completing the form, I immediately, like right away, receive an automatic notification thanking me for subscribing to the *Peter Gabriel Newsletter*. I've done it nine times so now I regularly receive nine emails at a time from you people.

Frankly, your insistence that Peter Gabriel is the sort of figure one would want news about is baffling and your efforts to retain me as a subscriber are a little pathetic. We both know that Peter Gabriel has become irrelevant to the music-buying, concert-attending public and that you folks have to resort to these tricks to maintain some form of subscriber base. I know how numbers get manipulated. I know how the stats get juked. I've seen *The Wire*. My ex-wife Christina and I used to regularly watch that show, which is centered around different forms of institutional malfeasance, so I know that your refusal to remove me from your mailing list has something to do with selling product, but also more to do with the data you provide to advertisers who determine revenue. I'm not stupid.

So, no, I am not interested in his new single, nor his upcoming tour. I do not like any of the music Peter Gabriel has produced. Not his work with Genesis, which I consider to belong to my parents' generation, not his ostentatious solo material, which I consider samey and overly produced. Not his so-called "groundbreaking" and "moving" movie scores, and especially not that crappy World Music he pretends to care about, which to me sounds like indigestion with a time signature.

The only song of his I can even stand is "Red Rain,"

which I will sometimes listen to all the way through without changing the channel when it comes on PYX 106, which is the classic rock radio station around here. "Solsbury Hill" is okay too, I guess.

Despite these exceptions, it is fair to say that I generally find Peter Gabriel's music distasteful and I would be happy to trade ever hearing those two decent songs ever again if it meant I was saved from the soulless carcass that is the rest of his catalog, particularly his late-career stuff. The melodramatic later work is what led to me first being placed on Mr. Gabriel's e-newsletter mailing list, so I have a particular distaste for that saccharine and heavy-handed stuff. My girlfriend at the time, Christina, who later became my wife, and then my ex-wife, loved some song about a father and child that Gabriel wrote and played an uncharacteristically spare and naked version of. She loved the black-and-white video where Gabriel emoted all over the keys of a piano and the lens of a camera. Her feelings toward this song had something to do with her own father and her, I am guessing.

I was never sure of the whole story. I never bothered to find out. Maybe I should have tried harder. Maybe if I had asked about her more often we would not have grown apart the way we did. Especially at the end there.

Or maybe she felt like the song would eventually have something to do with the children she imagined we would one day have. We were unable to have children, it turned out, which wasn't the sole cause of the end of our marriage, but it didn't help. Various factors go into ending a marriage, you know. Whether or not we could have children, and whose fault that was, were merely contributing factors to what was, by the point we realized we could not have babies together, an already hostile and unhealthy relationship.

She had some kind of grand expectation for me. There was some kind of mold I was supposed to fit into, the existence of which I was unaware when the relationship began. And this is unfair, I think. She was measuring me against other men. Against men she had previously dated, against her father, and her very successful older brothers. Maybe a pastor or some high school English teacher too, I can't be sure. The point is: she wanted me to be a certain way. She wanted me to be a good father to her as-yet-unborn child. I wasn't in any rush to be a dad and luckily, vis-à-vis our little fertility issue, I was never pushed into that role.

As far as I am concerned, and if I could be so bold, fathers are overrated anyway. Most people long for some relationship with their fathers, and if they don't have it they want some kind of reconciliation, but I don't. I don't see the point. When I watch a movie or a TV show where the father tragically dies and the child must avenge him or whatever, like in *The Lion King* or in pretty much any Batman movie, I always end up hating that movie. They are better off without a father as far as I am concerned. Without a father getting in the way, the kid has to learn to think for themself, and they can't be let down time and time again by some guy they wish was a hero, but who actually isn't.

But Christina was one of those people who wanted to reconcile with her father. He was the worst, though. Worked all the time, was never there for her, divorced her mom. All your classic bad dad stereotypes. Eventually she came to some kind of understanding with him. She was always trying to get me to go over there for Christmas and the like, and I just couldn't see why.

It just never made sense to me.

But I loved her. Even though I didn't try hard enough at being married, as they say. I didn't do all of the stuff I should have, I guess. I did the best I could though, and I used to do stuff for her all the time. Stuff like go to Christmas at her stupid dad's house with his new wife and all that. I would go over there in my dumb sweater and I would smile and be so polite and charming. Believe it or not, despite what you have seen in the various communications regarding, vis-à-vis, the newsletters you won't stop sending me, I can be very charismatic.

I also used to do other sweet stuff for her too, like rub her neck and feet and go to the store and buy maxi pads and all that other unromantic/romantic boyfriend-husband stuff. You know what I am talking about. The kind of stuff that when a guy in a TV show does it, you can tell he's a good guy. In real life guys don't actually get any credit for doing that stuff. Women tend to overlook those kinds of little annoyances and humiliations guys go through for them. On TV though you can tell very easily that the guy who ruins his favorite t-shirt painting the bathroom is the guy the girl is supposed to end up with, even though the guy is a little less handsome, and a little less cool than some other guy on the show played by Chris Messina or Dax Shepherd, or some jerk like that.

That is why I subscribed to your newsletter in the first place, as a matter of fact. Just because you bastards set it up so that you had to sign up for the newsletter in order to download that stupid goddamned father and son song from your website. I only did it because of Christina and her stupid dad. Because I am such a caring, charming, kindhearted damn guy. I would not have done it had I thought it would be so hard to unsubscribe from you bastards. I should have just let her do it with her own email account. She'd probably love getting these constant updates about where Peter Gabriel's next show is going to be and what musical endeavor he is working on. She probably still listens to him for all I know. I never understood why it appealed to her. Music is supposed to hit you in the gut. You know? It's supposed to mean something. It's supposed to be like an inside joke that only you and one other person get. Like that song by Lou Reed my dad used to love, or the one by Whiskeytown that Christina and I used to sing along to, or the one by The National that I can't even talk about right now. It's supposed to make you feel like it was written just for you, or just for you and one other person. Like you stumbled onto some deserted patch of beach that no one else has ever seen before. Peter Gabriel just doesn't do that for me. But it's not like I'm jealous of him or anything. It's not like I wish Christina would have romanticized the stuff I did as much as she romanticized the music of some washed-up pop star.

So, for all these reasons and a few more that I have not even mentioned here, I want you to remove me from your mailing list. You'll really be doing the both of us a favor because let me tell you: these tricks don't work. These little ploys and plans and plots. I know from experience. It's like, you think just because you leave stuff at your ex-wife's place you can keep going over there and she is going to fall in bed with you like that one time right around the 4th of July. But I can tell you right now, it is never going to be like it was. She is never gonna laugh in that way she used to laugh and tilt her head a little bit and offer you a beer.

So, if I have to accept that about Christina, then you need to accept that Peter God-Damned Gabriel is never gonna headline the MTV music awards again. Or the Grammies. Or whatever other stupid awards show they have now. And Peter, if you are reading this, you need to just deal with that reality. That time in your life is over. It's time to take a good, hard look in the mirror and try to figure out what you still have to offer and who is interested in it. Maybe you can take the knowledge and the skills you have and the love you once had for music and apply it to teaching young people how to unlock their potential. Has that ever crossed your mind, Peter? Or maybe there is a band you can contribute to who really needs your skill set. Like really needs it. Not like Genesis, who clearly didn't need you and who moved on so quickly after you left without even blinking an eyelash. Or maybe it has nothing to do with music at all. Who knows? Maybe you are an amazing gardener or something and you didn't even realize it.

But whatever you decide, first you need to move on. You have got to give up on the past. You have got to accept that you are in a new phase of your life now. You have to give yourself a break on mistakes you have made. It won't be easy, but you have to do it. For example, I never should have bought that Nissan. Nothing good ever came out of it. All it ever brought me was trouble. I know that now. I can see that. And after the divorce, when I went to Christina's dad's funeral, I realized that the things I was pissed about were petty. I couldn't even be there for

Christina when she needed me. It meant a lot to her that I came to the funeral and everything, but what was I supposed to say?

I can admit things like this to myself now. You should take a page out of my book because once you admit these things to yourself, you can finally move on. You can finally look to the future. You might be surprised by what you see out there. Maybe something even better is on the horizon.

I know you are going to keep emailing me. I know that you are going to send me newsletter updates for your new tour and your new record and I am going to get annoyed. I am going to froth at the mouth for a second and tell anyone who will listen how much I hate you. Who knows who I'll be saying it to, but whoever it is I will tell them, "Screw this guy and his music . . . " But I won't email you again. I really mean it this time. That would just be encouraging you.

Eventually, I won't even bother to delete the emails you send me. Every new Peter Gabriel E-Newsletter that you send me will sit with all the other 5,000 unread emails in my inbox that I skip over until I get to the ones from my mom, or old high school friends. I will change my email address one day because I will be updating my resume and trying to sound more professional and I will stop even looking at the one I was using when I made the mistake of subscribing to your newsletter so I could download that free song for my then-girlfriend, who became my wife, and who is now my ex-wife. You won't have my new address and all those emails you send will be like letters written to an old apartment, or phone calls made to a closed business. I'll have moved on. I am telling you all of this now, for your own good. I am telling you this now from the bottom of my heart: I really do want the best for you, Peter, but if you think that emailing me is going to make you happy, you are wrong. And the sooner you accept that, the happier you will be.

Yours truly, so sincere, and all that,

STRIP MALL, OR COGNIZING SIGNIFIERS IN RETAIL SERVICE SPACES

When I used to work at a massage parlor, this little dingleberry hanging off the ass of a strip mall no one went to anymore, I had to change my name. The reason I had to change my name was because when clients called the massage place and the owner read my real name from the availability list, a lot of people assumed I was a woman. I could always tell that was what they were thinking when I showed up in the Serenity Room with my dumb little mustache, my swoopy hair, and the shirtsleeves of my button-down rolled up.

These bulky guys would be sitting there all small and disappointed, trying to come up with an excuse to get out of having to be touched by me. I felt bad for them, I guess. So, I changed my name on the schedule to Marshall McLuhan and that worked well enough.

People know what a Marshall McLuhan is supposed to look like. I look like that, I guess. So, once I started using "Marshall McLuhan," people knew what to expect. That's how I met Barry. He just called up and asked for openings and they told him about me. "Marshall McLuhan has an opening at six," Claire probably told him, and he took it. Oh boy did he take it.

This all happened a long time ago. Years ago. Back before I was married. Back when my life was normal, when my girlfriend and I were having money problems and I needed to pick up extra jobs. I'd find cash gigs that wouldn't get taxed—shoveling driveways, walking dogs, and doing massages—to supplement the income from my main gig. My "real" job. You wanna know what my "real job" was? I was a lawyer, believe it or not. That's how we met, my girlfriend and me. We were both working for the same law firm. You are probably wondering why I needed extra yams if we were both lawyers. Well, they don't pay lawyers like you think they would. First off, it takes a long time to make partner and even then, they still try to fuck you. Even though we weren't making much more than an assistant manager at a big box electronics store, we were living the lives of young lawyers in the big city. Spending money like we hated it. And I guess we did.

I'm not sure how my girlfriend felt about me part-timing at a massage place, using friction and pressure to hustle up my half of the mortgage for our very-nice, too-expensive condo. We were usually in such bad moods all the time we hardly talked. She was part-timing too. Picking up extra shifts at the restaurant she worked at. We'd run into each other in the condo we were trying to keep, surprised to see one another. She'd be in the black and pink bathing suit she used to wear back when we used to play hooky from our lives and go down to the beach together when the weather got nice.

That's what she wore to work, believe it or not. That pink and black bathing suit. She worked at this place called the Pool House. It was one of those restaurants where the waitresses walked around half-naked. You know the kind of place. It was the kind of place where the Os on the sign in the word POOL wore a bikini top. This place was pool themed, so they wore these headsets that looked like snorkels and they were allowed to wear whatever bathing suit to work they wanted. So that's why she would be wearing that black and pink one-piece all the time. I say it was a one-piece but it actually showed off more than most bikinis. She got a lot of tips, but not as many as you might think for as much skin as she showed. Sometimes my brother would ask me how I felt about her working there, with all those dudes drooling all over her pillows. But I told him I didn't really care. I didn't even really like those places.

So, there we were, stuck working these shitty jobs in this strip mall no one went to anymore. We had to get those jobs or we'd end up losing our very-nice, too-expensive condo. We'd end up living in a reasonably priced duplex on the train line with a washer-dryer in the basement and whoever heard of a couple lawyers living in a place like that? We weren't raised lower-middle class. Or even middle-middle class. Getting kicked out of the condo and ending up in a duplex just wasn't who we were. Leave that to those other fuckers. So that's how I ended up working at the massage parlor.

She was the one who told me about the place. My girlfriend.

"You could be a masseuse," she'd told me one day after work. By the way she said it, I couldn't tell if she was joking or not. She was still in that pink and black bathing suit that she was wearing, but not for me. "The place in the strip mall is looking for people."

"Don't you need to be certified?" I'd asked her.

"It's called Mediums & Massages. Can you even deal with it?" she'd said, thrilled at the absurdity of the gimmick.

The place sounded so dumb, so freaking stupid, that I just had to check it out.

"So, you, like, tell fortunes, or whatever?" I asked the owner when I showed up for my interview. I didn't understand at first, but Claire explained it to me. That was the owner's name. Claire. Claire Voiant. I don't think it was her real name, but I guess you never know.

She was very pretty, but in a completely abstract way. Even though she wasn't married, she looked like somebody's once-upon-a-time trophy wife who'd moved into the executive phase of her marriage. Her shirts were immaculate.

There was a faux intimacy about the way she interacted with other people. She hunkered down and furrowed her brow when you talked, but she was merely affecting a pose. She was so assured I couldn't tell if she was a great huckster or if she really believed in it all. She talked with a convert's enthusiasm; a born-again fervor that flushed her cheeks and urged her eyes to the front of her sockets. She utilized jargon like "energy vampire" and "solar plexus," "throat chakra" and "tuning fork." It didn't seem like it was going well until I told her I was going to lose my condo. She wrapped her fingers around my wrist and looked me in the eyes.

"I get it," she said. "I'm trying to save this place as well. Why don't you help yourself by helping me?"

I didn't know what to say to that so I just nodded.

"I'm so excited for you," she told me and then made

me sign a contract to rent a space from her. It was a rental situation. I was supposed to bring in my own clients, of course. I didn't but there was enough business that they could just throw people to me, the people who called. People like Barry. Subcontracting was basically a way for Claire to take a cut of what we earned. That was her main deal. The rent we paid to her. There wasn't enough money in just massages, I guess. Or in communicating with the dead.

The reason she wanted us to be independent, 1099-form contractors was financial, of course, but she also liked having the distance. So, like, when Trudy got into it with one of the customers, or the cops came around looking to shake us down for illicit sex acts, she could act like we were mercenary yahoos whose names she hardly even knew. Other times, though, when she was trying to enact some new protocol, she talked to us like the general of some army in which we'd all enlisted. Like when she banned us all from using the term "empathic" with clients and then later when she changed her mind and insisted that we use the term at least one time in every session. Or how we weren't allowed to call ourselves masseuses or masseurs or even massage specialists because she made us call ourselves mediums. Language was very important to her. Mainly she wanted us to pretend to have special powers. I was supposed to talk to the ancestors of my clients while I kneaded the muscle tissue of their thoracic regions.

"We're not psychics," Claire would say.

"So should I get a Ouija board?" I asked her.

"That's ghosts. We talk to spirits," she said but I didn't know the difference.

"I don't know what to tell them," I told Claire.

"You don't tell them anything. You just have to listen to the spirits and repeat what it is you hear them say."

"But I don't hear spirits."

"Spirits talk to us in many different ways."

"What kinds of things do spirits say?" I asked, hoping she'd divulge the script.

"Just try to tell the client something they already know," she said and still I couldn't tell if she was being profound or copping to the grift.

"It's just a gimmick," Trudy told me later while we smoked in the alley on our lunch break. "It's just a way to get their attention."

Trudy really got into the gimmick though. She bought a crystal ball from a gift shop and wore drooping, slinking shawls, cheap beads dripping off them like some gypsy. I know that's not okay to say anymore, but that's what she looked like. The image you have of a gypsy.

She was right, though. Most people didn't expect us to have magic powers. A lot of people just used it as a way to try to get a handy. "Can you get a reading on if I'll ever be . . . happy?" they would ask, their eyebrows creeping up in altitude like a roller-coaster reaching its apex. And it's not that I couldn't tell what they wanted from the beginning. It's not like it wasn't obvious.

It wasn't all the guys though. Some guys wanna get jerked off, don't get me wrong, but not every guy. I don't know what the ratio is for the women who worked there, but for me it was kind of a 60 / 40 type of situation.

Those guys who would come in looking for something like that, something extra let's call it, they tipped poorly too. Though one guy, who I was sure wanted a handy, tipped exorbitantly after I finished his standard massage.

As much as, I assume, he would have tipped had I jerked him off. To alleviate the guilt maybe? Then I never saw him again. I never saw any of those dudes again. They came in, dropped their shitty tip, and never came back. They were testing me I guess, trying to discover something about me. And once they did, once they found out, they were gone.

It wasn't technically a proposition. It was more of a feeling-out process. No one ever asked for one outright. But there were little signs. Little movements. A nervous energy. A story that didn't quite add up about "feeling stressed" about work or a sports injury that seemed unlikely. And then there was the squirming. The little vocalizations. The need their body would throw off like a scent. There was a quality to it. Almost like heat. Almost like a color. They wouldn't be using their real name either. I would read their name off the schedule while they sat in the Serenity Room and they wouldn't even look up.

"Are you Charles?" I would ask, standing right in front of them. I would have to get down in a squat, look them in the face and speak their fake name at them before they would finally remember and quickly stand up as if caught and they would follow me back to a session room. The two of us would be in there pretending to be "Charles" and "Marshall McLuhan," and they would pretend they wanted a massage and nothing else and I would pretend not to notice their erection.

Maybe it wasn't 60%. Sometimes it seemed like 60%, though.

Whatever the ratio, anyone who wasn't trying to get a hand job was pretty much all old people who no one would touch anymore. Divorced men, crusty and grey.

Widows. I had a burn victim once. I'd like to say he was a really nice guy and we had a special connection, but he was just kind of aloof and sad. He looked apologetic when I came into the Serenity Room to bring him back to the massage room for our session.

"They are talking to me from the other side," I reported to him as I ran my hands over his raised flesh. "They say there was a fire, but they are okay now. They are at peace."

He nodded like he knew I was going to say that and then he left. He was living some whole other movie and I was hardly a character in it.

My brother had this whole other conception of the place. He used to tell me how lucky I was that I got paid to "rub oil on all these chicks," but the place wasn't what he thought.

"Do you tell them that the ghosts want them to suck your dick?" he whispered into the phone. I could tell he was hiding the conversation from his wife and that made it worse for me.

"That would be a violation," I told him. "Of something. Everything, actually."

"I'd be jerking off in between every one," he would say to me, unable to contain his verve. He'd hiss his fantasies into the phone until his wife knocked on the bathroom door and asked him what he was doing in there.

"I'm talking to my brother," he'd bark at her, louder than anything he'd said throughout the entire conversation, then he'd go right back to whispering to me. "Do you ever give them a towel that's too small to cover their boobs and their vag?"

But it wasn't like that. At least not for me. I never told

him that almost all my clients were men. I never did tell him about Barry.

There were female clients, of course, but most of the women were the type who took up two chairs with their coat and bag when they sat in the waiting room. The type who would show up unshowered in a stiff, loose sweatshirt, the type who don't even know enough to be embarrassed by their scent.

You'd think if they knew they were going to get touched they would shower and come in smelling like soap or deodorant, but not these women. Not my clientele. In the mornings it wasn't too bad, but by evening? Well, I can assure you that everyone stinks once the sun goes down, especially these folks.

They had skin tags. They would cough when I touched them. They had rough patches on their elbows, ribs that stuck out wild from their flanks. They would lay there like a cooked, pink ham, waiting for the knives.

"Your father says he is proud of you," I would say, and they would nod, unsurprised by the information.

"You will come into a large sum of money," I would tell them, but their mind would already be made up about the tip.

"I guess someone got murdered here," Trudy told me once when we were having our smoke.

"How do you know that?" I asked, looking around for a presence.

"Claire," she said and took a drag. "And one of the ghosts."

"Stop," I told her. I didn't want her to know she was freaking me out, but she knew.

"It was a gangland killing."

"Are we in the gangland?"

"No. That's just what they call it when someone gets killed behind some mob stuff."

"The dead guy was in the mob?"

"No. He was black, but the mob killed him."

"They shot him?"

"The weird thing was he didn't even come in for a massage. He just came in here to hide, but they found him."

"How long ago was this?"

"Not that long ago."

So many of the guys who came in to get a massage had come straight from the Pool House. They came in looking defiant, like we were going to try to deny them. Or expectant, like we were just another item on the menu from the place. Like you could order wings, beers, and a hand job.

They never had appointments. We were an impulse purchase like those sunglasses and batteries and bags of candy they sell you when you are in line at the grocery store. They hummed, swollen with the weak beers my girlfriend had sold them at the other end of the strip mall. They wandered down and discovered the masseuses and masseurs of Mediums & Massages like some kind of sex oasis. You could always tell who'd broken off from their friend-group and gone looking for some shameful comfort, some semi-legal form of satisfaction. They stunk, dully.

I was always afraid of finding breast cancer. Trudy had a knack for it. It was like the tumor found her. It really freaked her out. Freaked me out too. The first time she found one she told the woman and it damn near wrecked them both. She tried to tell them the spirits revealed it to her, but she couldn't keep up the façade and she just helped her find the lump. It somehow made it worse.

Poor Trudy spent the rest of the day locked in the bathroom sobbing. After that, if she ever found a tumor, she wouldn't mention it to the client. What was she supposed to do? It's not like she was a breast doctor. "Your husband says he misses you," she would say as she rubbed her fingers over the site of the metastasizing cells. She would tell me though. And then she just wouldn't take those women's appointments. I never found it on anyone but any time I started with a client I always wondered if I would. There was always that moment of anxiety before I touched them.

Barry came in a couple times a month and he wore jeans and a Dickies shirt and a Carhartt coat. Most people figure the guys who get a massage (a for real massage and not just a happy ending) are yoga doofuses—soft hands, man-bun hair, nice shoes—but that's not how it was. This guy, Barry, his flesh was hard. Like a shell. With some people it was like pressing rotten fruit when I rubbed them, but with Barry I had to claw through it with my elbow. His stumpy, hard fingers were like the roots of a small tree, grabbing the earth. The muscles on his back were big and hard, like piles of rocks beneath his flesh. He wasn't a bodybuilder though. I had a bodybuilder for a while, actually. He was an okay client. Not the best tipper. Spent most of the session complaining about his hemorrhoids. Once he saw Trudy he switched to her account for good. It was fine. She was the best one anyway. Plus he farted a lot.

Most guys fart while in session, though. It's pretty common. They would usually try to pretend like it didn't happen, but I would always notice. I could tell what was wrong with them by their farts. If they drank too much, snorted cocaine, if they weren't getting enough sleep.

Most men stink. Whether they fart or not, they stink.

"The spirits are showing me something . . . Some kind of party, maybe?"

A lot of times when clients farted it grossed me out, but somehow with Barry—I'm getting back to Barry again—I didn't mind. Not only did I not mind, I worried he would feel bad about it; get self-conscious. I wished there was a way for me to tell him that it didn't bother me when he did it, which wasn't even that often. Just sometimes. Not that his farts didn't stink, cuz they did—stank like maybe he had something wrong with his kidneys—but we were doing something together. Working on something. Working together to achieve something, so I didn't mind that much about his farts and I didn't want him to worry about it.

And he didn't expect me to give him some dumb fortune either. We never even talked about it. It never came up. The reason I remember him, though, the reason I liked him so much, was he let me do whatever I wanted to him. He really let me dig in and go all the way. Try everything. A lot of guys pretended they were tough, but they couldn't take the pressure I offered. They hissed and sucked in their breath, winced a little like a kid falling off his bike. They talked to me like I'd done something wrong, backed into their Mercedes or something.

"I thought this was supposed to be a medium massage," they would say.

"It's not that kind of medium," I would tell them.

They were pained by my pressure, but also shamed for not being able to take it. It would be a nuisance for us both to play our little parts in that drama; that it had been I who was wrong and not they who were weak. But not with Barry. He just took every elbow, every deep tissue technique I could throw at him.

When we were done, he would look at me like it had all been nothing more than a slight inconvenience. Which was kind of funny to me. That the massage that he scheduled and paid for was sort of a hassle for him. He looked at me like I was making him do it. But I didn't mind because he had just spent the previous fifty minutes meeting the deepest pressure I could offer with nothing more than a grunt, a wheezing sigh into the head pillow.

"I bet you can smell their pussy," my brother whispered into the phone. I could hear his kids shouting at each other, his wife cursing at them. "When you massage them?"

"I bought a new car," I said.

"Can you afford that?" he asked. I hated when he said stuff like that. Sensible, rational stuff. I wanted him to get back to fake tits and finger blasting.

"No," I admitted. "I can't really afford it."

"You are just like Mom," he said, satisfied.

"You are just like Mom," I told him.

"What kind of car is it?"

"I'm not sure. It was expensive though. It has the engine sticking out of the hood."

"You live downtown. You don't even need a car."

"The train stops running at two though."

"You are gonna lose that condo, bro. And your fiancée is gonna leave you."

"We're not engaged yet," I said, kind of annoyed because I knew he was probably right.

"And they are gonna repossess that car."

I knew he was right about that too and I hoped they did because no matter where I parked it, I always got a ticket and I was always paranoid someone was going to scratch it if they saw it because that's what I would do if I saw a car like that.

"Do you ever think about Mom?"

"No," I said. Then I thought about it and I said, "No."

One day Barry came in and he wasn't wearing his wedding ring. I noticed but didn't say anything. I didn't want him to think I was trying to be his bartender or anything like that. And we never talked to each other much anyway. We didn't have that kind of relationship.

"My wife left me," he said at the end of the session, and he held his hand up like it was a prop in a movie. Like the hand didn't belong to him and he was talking about some other schmuck whose wife had left him and who had yanked his ring off his finger in a fit of rage and tossed it down the toilet or out the window or whatever you do when you pull a wedding ring off your finger. "She's got the kids," he said.

"Yeah," I said, like I already knew.

He sighed deeply, his lungs sounding congested, like ice slipping across the roof.

When we left the session room and started walking back to the Serenity Room, Barry took the lead unexpectedly. I usually led the client out, like they were some kid being marched to the principal's, but his admission wrested control of the session from me. Like, now that he had learned that marriages end, none of the other rules applied. I tried to think of what to say to him about his wife and his ring and all that. I thought about telling him my real name, but I didn't. I followed him down the hall, past the front desk and toward the exit. I watched him cross the parking lot of the strip mall and walk into the Pool House. He went after his massage and there was something about that that was just polite. Something about that that I respected.

I saw him one other time after that. Claire came and knocked on the door to the session room I was in. I'd been sleeping, but she didn't know that.

"There's someone here to see you," she said.

"In the Serenity Room?" I asked.

"At the front desk," she said and then she disappeared in a puff of lavender-scented steam.

When I got to the front desk, the wife was standing there. I could tell it was the wife, just by the way she looked at me. Just by the sad, lonely hollow in her eyes. And because Barry's ghostly form was floating there nude behind her, his unfinished business keeping him suspended in the air, like snowflakes in a streetlight that scatter but won't come down.

That was the day I started seeing ghosts for real. All of them, not just Barry. I started seeing the tired-looking woman who Trudy found cancer on, a construction worker buried when ground was broken on the strip mall decades earlier, Claire's first husband.

"Barry's dead," the wife said. The bullet wound gaped his head open, bigger in the back than it was in the front, but I was more surprised to find that Barry had been his real name.

"I see," I said and what she didn't know was that I meant it literally, that I was looking right at his split-apart skull.

"I just wanted you to know that I know."

"That he's dead?"

He left when she did, following behind her like a scolded puppy, but the rest of the ghosts didn't. They remained, trying to haunt the massage place but haunting me instead. The cancer victims, dead and breastless, abandoned children screaming and suckling at nothing, the ghosts of erect men destined to carry their blue balls into the afterlife, and the black guy the mob killed not so long before I started.

That's how I found the money. The black guy, scared and nude, his lips chapped and cracked, searched the wall with his fingers, pressing against the soggy gypsum. I followed him into one of the session rooms and pulled away the wall with my bare hands to discover what the guy was trying to hide from the mob. He looked at me the way Claire had when I told her that I was trying to save my condo. He looked at me the way Barry did when he talked about his wife. He looked at me the way my brother did when he talked about his high school football team.

And so that's how Barry helped me get my life together. I was flush with the cash I needed to save our condo. I married my girlfriend and she quit the Pool House. She never wore that pink and black bathing suit for me again, but at least she stopped wearing it for all those Barrys who came in to stare at her pillows.

I thought when I quit Mediums & Massages that the ghosts would disappear, but it got worse. I got a white noise machine to try to drown out the sound of the spirits, gone but not, full of desire but incapable of getting. The machine was supposed to sound like the ocean, but it sounded like a paper bag being wrinkled and unwrinkled over and over again for eternity.

There I'd be in my office, sound machine crackling away, studying case law, reviewing pleadings, reading statute changes—I wasn't one of those trial lawyers you see on television—and I'd be surrounded by everyone's past, the mistakes people long dead had made, their desires palpable and embarrassing. I couldn't drown them out so I put them to work, having them tell me what clients couldn't or wouldn't. It was a good little hustle. I started working more hours, taking on more case files than anyone else, got on the partner track. It wasn't as hard as I thought it would be. All I needed to do was find fifty grand hidden in a wall, work eighty hours a week, and start talking to ghosts.

My brother would ask me about the firm at Thanksgiving.

"I bet chicks love it when you tell them you're a partner, don't they?" he'd whisper while we stood out back in the cold so he could sneak a cigarette.

"I guess," I told him and tried not to look at our dead cousin who dangled nude and invisible to him, fifteen and slack jawed.

"How many girlfriends do you have?" he wanted to

know.

"I don't know how to answer that," I told him.

"You can't even keep track," he squealed, delighted, and he punched me so hard on the shoulder that I had to brush my teeth with my left hand for a week.

So here I am, toiling away in my office, my real name on one of those little nameplate plaques in the middle of my desk, white noise machine cranked all the way up trying to drown out the sounds of my co-workers' dead parents, a cop who was killed in the line of duty, the ghosts of migrants deceased from sickness, and a whole bunch of others. When people ask me if anything is wrong, if everything is okay, I tell them, "You bet. I own a private jet. Everything is swell." When they ask me about my wife, I tell them what they want to hear, whatever lie they need to hear so we can all get through our day.

A PAINTING OF SUCH REPUTATION

I had no intention of reviewing Camilla Rowland's installation, the one prominently (and dare I say, proudly) featured at the center of the Midwest Center for Art's current exhibit, but my relationship with the piece known as "Exultation of Inconsistency" is too well known for me to escape without comment. People have asked me about it with impressively unremitting frequency over the past several years, and I can only assume that interrogation will continue. They ask about that painting when I am on panels, they inquire about the intention of Rowland's use of line when I lecture at universities, they ask in private about the composition when I am cornered at cocktail parties or while I try to urinate during the intermission of a performance of Haydn's "The Creation." Indeed, the primary reaction to the release of my book last year, a grouping of essays collected from a decades-long career as—I don't mind telling you since I long ago learned how corrosive false modesty can be—one of the most prominent and respected art critics of the generation, was a near-universal roar of objection that there had been no juicy details about my long-standing relationship and semi-public falling out with the sometimes lauded, sometimes criticized piece that Camilla Rowland (or as I knew her, Cammy) painted midway through her unorthodox career. I don't know if this is the time or the venue to describe my relationship with the work of art, or associated parties like Cammy and the infamous Doris Moore, but this publication has generously bequeathed this space to me, and I have decided to use it to set the record straight, so to speak. Whether or not this is ill-advised remains to be seen. This piece of writing will be my final word on this entire matter, and no one will be responding on my behalf to any further comments on it by any party.

I first became aware of the painting called "Exultation of Inconsistency," not unlike everyone else, at Camilla Rowland's show at the Transnational, which I attended as a very young man. She had just come scurrying back to oils and the canvas after a string of failures, and she needed to present herself as a general in the army of Neo-Anti-Traditionalism, marshaling her forces for the war against the fad that was Anti-Neo-Modernism. While I had been earning my degree, Rowland was revered, written about in our textbooks like she was some kind of geographic anomaly. By the time I was writing for the arts section of *The Dragoon* I had already witnessed the once lauded painter's collapse—those dark performance art days, dressed as a stuffed animal, blooming like a pustule on security camera footage; listed in the liner notes on the record of a deconstructionist synthwave band as playing "thoughts & prayers"; the incident with the acetylene torch when she was trying to become a sculptor.

I see now that these flights of fancy, these forays into art forms where she didn't belong, are part of what makes us love her, part of why we find her so troublingly intoxicating, so delightfully problematic. It was these incursions into realms where she was ill-equipped for success that engendered her oils on canvas with such life once she returned.

So, I knew of her, thought I understood her even, when I was sent over to that show, *The Void Staring Back: Survey of Line, Light, and Thought.* My attendance had been offered as some kind of olive branch between my institution and the gallery owner, the details of the row never being revealed to me. I wasn't even there to see Rowland's work, however. That wasn't even the point of it. I was there to see Parker Joyce Synge's sculptures, fire-kilned madness that they were. And we all know where she ended up.

The show failed to engage me at first—it was one of those events that had beautiful caterers but terrible food—and under that malaise I found myself looking for an exit. It was when I stepped outside that I saw the painting; "Exultation of Inconsistency" and all those lurid colors vibrating from the canvas the way steel does when it's wet. That piece, erroneously labeled by most casual observers with the outdated descriptor of "abstract," stood there rebelling against the wind, chatting up some busker in the light left behind by the setting sun, pretending that he wasn't trying to score some cocaine, though he was very obviously trying to score some cocaine.

To be clear, and for those of you who don't know (I don't know why you might be reading this if you don't already know), "Exultation of Inconsistency" is anthropomorphic. He has no mouth to speak, yet he speaks. He has no esophagus to swallow, yet he swallows. He has no organs with which to reproduce, yet he makes love. Just like you might. Curious, no?

I interrupted the anthropoid painting and the timid busker, asking for a light. The busker hustled off, and "Exultation of Inconsistency" spoke to me. The painting introduced himself as Jessie, as if the work was separate from him as an entity, as if "Exultation of Inconsistency" was just some part he played in a long-closed play. I didn't question the moniker since most of the people I'd gone to school with had either contorted their first name into a single initial that adorned their middle name like a designer handbag, or simply asked to be credited in their articles for major Art & Culture magazines as "Spike" or the digit "4."

I could tell upon first seeing Jessie that if he wasn't good, there was at least something I liked about him. Rowland's work during that period had evolved to the point where line and color achieved a sort of grace she'd never approached before, but that wasn't what made the painting so attractive. There was something different about him, unique. He was not completely original, of course, he would not exist were it not for Rothko and Duchamp, but who among us isn't the descendant of someone or something? And just because you can trace my ancestry back to someone who traded slaves, was a Nazi sympathizer, and who gouged rural farmers during the Great Depression, I'd petition you not to utilize that information to formulate expectations for me.

Camilla found us out in the alleyway, stifled in our efforts to acquire cocaine and having settled for sertraline provided by a fellow gallery attendee instead. Camilla hustled us back inside, tsking and clucking so ferociously like she always used to. At the time, it was unclear if her Exultation series was going to matter, and she didn't want it to get away from her, so I couldn't blame her for ruining our fun and nannying us back into the gallery.

We couldn't know that "Exultation of Inconsistency" would come to be known as the defining work of the artist, as well as the series, and eventually post-anarcho-brutalism in general. I think I was blind to it all because Jessie was the first good time I'd had in a while. We spent the rest of the showing making fun of the artists, trying to start a fire in the bathroom, and talking about our mutual interest in the Mandelbrot set. In short, we liked each other from the start, attracted to each other's propensity for mischief and the shared knowledge that we were so much more helically enlightened than everyone else and all their terrestrial concerns. I couldn't know what was to come. I couldn't expect the Doris Moore situation to unfold. I was focused on progressing in the world of art criticism, having my voice heard and my opinions matter.

My initial review went something like this:

> The work is lustful and virile, potent and dumb. It has the decency to not be beautiful, but it finds a way to lord that over you. It perseverates on the absurd. On the obtuse. It knows better, and it knows it knows better. What can be more obnoxious? Still, it would make a lovely dinner guest. Full of knowledge and anecdotes, an off-kilter sensibility and the desire to do right. To make good on some promise. To thumb its nose at convention and to try to transcend, though what it attempts to transcend is anyone's guess.

The review was hesitant but effective. Along with Geary's description of the textures being "treacherous" and Weingartner's suggestion that the tone was "welcome," my article helped to establish the work in the scene. I wasn't the only one to notice Jessie or comment on him, of course. One choice line that came out of that very show, and one that I see quoted over and over again (and it will be easy enough for you to track down who said it) is, "Though the form may be inconsequential, the line work gives the piece an import its brethren in the movement do not typically possess." Critics often suffer under the delusion that if you compliment someone or something, it's like you are the one who did the thing. I don't mean to be so critical of my fellow cultural assessors, but after being a part of a class for so long, one can't help but develop opinions.

Cammy was thrilled with all of this, of course, and so she used the goodwill earned by the successful show to run off to the field of robotics, deeming it the most relevant form in the art world before returning defeated to the easel and palate. I didn't think about the artist, the venue, or the work again until I encountered Jessie sometime later and quite by chance. I found him, of all places, at the Y on 79th and Bentham. He was talking to a big fellow who was getting dressed, and "Exultation of Inconsistency" was making a fool out of himself, as usual.

"That trainer you were talking to was unbelievable," Jessie said. "Great body. Is she through the gym?"

"What trainer?" the big fellow asked.

"In the red tank top. And the yoga pants?"

"That's my fiancée," the man replied and slammed his locker. His nose was twisted, and when he slammed the locker I noticed the chisel of his pecs. The ceiling bulbs created a jagged chiaroscuro contrast between each twitching muscle of his body.

"Jessie," I said, surprising both the annoyed Adonis and the 55.125" x 65.125" acrylic and oil on sewn silk, cotton, and linen with colors that Limpidi called "lurid," but Ng had suggested were "enlightened." I don't know if Jessie recognized me, but he was happy that his conversation was being redirected so soon after sticking his metaphorical foot in his mouth. Though he had no foot, of course. Since he was a painting.

We went out for lunch at that place near the Y that no one goes to anymore, the Vaguely Cajun Café where I had a bowl of Pretty Much Gumbo, and he had a sandwich they called a Destitute Male Child. That place has lost most of its charm by now, though it's still there in some form or another. We ate our lunch, and that, of course, turned into drinks. Well, I drank. It turned out he didn't drink alcohol, preferring teas or simply water. We had something of an odd but enjoyable night—finding venues we'd never seen before or since, encountering folks with sensibilities so charmingly off-kilter that they didn't seem real, getting invited into environs because of how we were and what we looked like. We laughed derisively and acceptingly through most of it.

Jessie was self-satisfied and strange, opinionated about the most obscure things. He could sometimes be difficult, but I found that I liked him quite a bit. He had nice things to say about the artist who painted him, but also honest things. The type of things that didn't usually come up. "Cammy is preoccupied with her feet. In ways that I think go beyond hygiene . . . " and "The woman doesn't excuse herself after she farts. It's the strangest thing I've ever seen." And he flattered me as well. In a way that seemed genuine. He seemed, at the time, to be quite transparent. Uninterested in hiding anything. He talked openly about his negative opinion of his own appearance, his complex relationship with the opposite sex, his mother. I felt like I was in the presence of authenticity. That was my mistake.

We spent a lot of time together over the next few years. Parties, late-night conversations at bistros I didn't know existed, even over the phone or via text. I introduced Jessie to people. Young artists who I thought might fall in love with one or the other of us; people who I thought might be impressed by my knowing the painting; frustrated mid-careerists whom I thought he might help. Because of my relationship with Jessie, and a few other works it doesn't seem necessary to mention here, my reputation grew. Though I reject the term "kingmaker," gendered and regressive as it is, I will admit to a certain amount of clout in the art and even the literary and cinematic worlds—not too bad for a kid from upstate who always dreamed of the exquisite corpse that is the skyline of Manhattan. If one were to be magnanimous to Jessie, one might attribute some of my success to him. Being one of the first to notice him gave me a bit of clout and gravitas that would shield me from later missteps (the less said about *Analogic Effervescent* and the Josiah Twins the better.)

Jessie changed as well. No longer just an objet d'art, he was now a dandy-about-town, earning friends within my social circle and without. He once introduced me to a Croatian freedom fighter whom I found charming and a bit sinister. You never knew who you'd find Jessie with.

Once he overcame the expectation that he be given the kind of clout he received hanging on a wall and once he navigated the inconvenience of being a canvas on a wooden frame, plastered with paint and having no hands, feet, digestive tract, sex organs, or legally recognized personhood, he found his way in the world quite well.

Because of my proximity to Jessie, I got into places I had no business being, I had a sense of self-assuredness that I did not deserve. I broke laws and was not held accountable. I felt bulletproof. We all did. It seemed like we were doing something big together. Like there was some destiny compelling us. I wasn't so naïve as to think we would change the world with art, but I thought we might make some kind of impact. I thought that, between Camilla, Doris Moore, Jessie, and me, we were the start of something. That things would change after us. That we were different. That the normal rules wouldn't apply to us. But it turned out we were just like everybody else. Just petty and mean and ruled by our passions. And discovering that together made us hate one another.

The falling-out happened around the time Camilla died. Maybe that was part of it. The work seemed different without her. More permanent. Hallowed, somehow. For a long time I used to put Jessie in the same category as other works I considered important: the photography of Walker Evans, Andy Warhol's disquieting portrait of JonBenét Ramsey, Bouguereau's *Satyr Drowned by Nymphs*, and the entirety of the work of Richard Brautigan. We all have a funny way of curating the museums we keep in our hearts.

I don't even care about the money he owes me anymore. I don't even hold it against him that he thinks I was trying to sleep with his wife. The infamous Doris Moore situation that everyone always asks about. And, at this point, it is important to clarify, precisely because there has been so much talk, so much rumor swirling around this situation, that I did not have an affair with Jessie's wife—didn't sleep with her, anyway. Doris, feline, disorganized, and lewd, and I, pompous, self-aggrandizing, mean, had both been not only seduced by Jessie but also convinced of the notion of a beauty beyond the norm, of the absurdity of the mores and expectations of the day. Jessie's mysticism enthralled us.

It's true, of course, that Doris and I did spend more time together than anyone else associated with the neo-paleo-fundamentalists. And we didn't tell Jessie how often we got together. How could we? He'd have just been fine with it, and who would want that? We wanted to cuckold him with our chaste friendship, getting off on not getting off. The delicious thrill of asking if the other had mentioned the lunch date at Geryon's to him and confirming that we hadn't. Hand-waving away notions of infidelity with the flimsy proof that we'd never seen one another nude.

We did not love one another. At least I didn't love her. She might have felt differently; it's not my place to speak for her. You'd have to ask her if perhaps she longed for me to provide for her the things Jessie could not. You'd have to ask her that. As for what you can ask me, I suppose you could ask if I feel guilty, and I do. I know that I could have handled the whole thing differently. I know the ways in which I erred, and I will have to be the one who lives with those mistakes.

The last time I saw him was at the Dilettante, where Doris and I liked to meet for drinks. We were chatting up some teen chess prodigy who was there drinking club soda, trying to get served. We'd both turned down lunch offers from Jessie that day, lighting upon some excuse or another, always surprising ourselves with how easy it was to deceive him, how simple, how willing he was to believe. We laughed about it when we got together.

"He just thinks that people run off to meet with their genealogist in the middle of the day."

"Can you imagine being that oblivious?"

When we looked up from our mirth, we saw all those textures Anton Geary had described as "treacherous" and the color selection Kline had suggested was "enlightened."

"Are you enjoying yourselves," Jessie said to us, chasing off the chess child. He knew just where to find us. He always had. "You two look like the worst couple since Brando fucked Dick Pryor."

Doris didn't take the bait. She never did. When Camilla had been with us, Camilla and Doris would scurry away to laugh about Russian composers and other inside jokes that they found uproarious but that Jessie and I didn't care to get. Without Camilla to distract her, Doris looked long and hard at Jessie, waiting obediently for the next insult.

"Sit down with us," I offered, though I knew it was the wrong thing to say.

"Did you think I wouldn't find out?" he asked her before I could even pull out a chair.

"I hoped you would," she told Jessie.

"Would you just sit down?" I said, trying not to plead.

"She knows what this is about," Jessie said, without sitting.

Doris' mouth was a citrus fruit unplucked, her arms

folded as tight as an envelope.

"I wish you'd told me she was trash when you introduced us," Jessie said.

"I think you introduced me to her," I corrected, though I wasn't sure.

"It's not like it was anything that you haven't done," she said.

"I thought we were past that," he said.

"I guess I wasn't past it," she said to him, her arms still stuck to each other, her lips still pursed.

Then Jessie said something that I'll never forget. Something so despicable that I can't even relate it here. We all sat silent after Jessie said it, looking at one another, wondering what we were to do now.

"Maybe we should go," I said.

"Did you know about this?" Jessie asked me.

And, of course, I knew about the affairs. All of them. I knew who everyone was sleeping with. What could I say? What did he think we talked about while we were gadding from one overpriced rooftop bistro to the next? Even that wouldn't have been the end if it weren't for the stick-up. We'd fought like that before, betrayed one another. It wasn't abnormal.

I didn't think anything bad could happen when I was with Jessie. Nothing really bad. I thought that knowing Jessie was going to save me from something, anything, everything. I thought knowing him would matter. So when the chess kid turned out to be a stick-up artist, the pimply kid transformed into a menace by the same magic that had animated Jessie and made us all, no one thought anything would go wrong. So when the chess-prodigy-cum-stick-up-kid pulled his gun on us, no one took him seriously until he killed the bartender. That's when we filled a bag with our valuables.

"I'm gonna shoot someone else," he said, like he was confessing it. "Who's it gonna be?"

"Don't . . . " Doris said when he turned his gun on Jessie. "Shoot me instead."

"Anything to say about that, fella?" the stick-up artist who maybe could have been the next Kasparov (or maybe the next Dillinger) wanted to know.

Jessie didn't say anything. He shook his head and turned his will and his fate over to the boy.

So that was pretty much the end of things. Jessie and I weren't friends after that. None of us were. How could we be? The old chess-prodigy-as-a-disguise-for-a-stick-up-kid routine. We should have seen it coming. Though it wouldn't have mattered. Something else would have led us to that dissolution point eventually. We all moved on in some form. The stick-up kid went to jail, and the bartender went to the morgue; Jessie returned, Dorisless, to his position in the museum—the wooden frame and canvas hanging on the wall, the line-work as resplendent as ever; Doris went back to composing, never to speak to either of us again; Cammy is dead, of course; and I have become the specimen you have come to know and trust.

I see now that maybe Jessie and I were just in the right place at the right time. That perhaps we needed each other for either of us to have any meaning. But who knows if that's right. This all happened a long time ago.

So, seeing that "Exultation of Inconsistency," that painting of such renown, is at the Midwestern Center for the Arts brings back a lot of memories. Some good, some bad. It would have been nice to see Camilla again, sipping wine, her makeup not quite right, the redolent sense that she had somewhere else to be. But she is long dead, of course. I wonder what she would have thought about how Jessie had changed. No longer as piercing, the garde that he was the avant of having been relieved of duty and relegated to context for that new wave, the Retro-Proto-Classicists or the Meta-Radical-Minimalists and then whatever comes after that. Not that it matters what she would have thought of him. Despite the years, there is still something about him. Something beautiful and charming, tragic and humble, but I've learned too much since first seeing him. I've become myself and no longer need to wonder what I was in context to him. It is bittersweet to say goodbye to the kind of fear and excitement that blooms in a new relationship. But there are new feelings associated with the letting go. New cavities created by releasing the hold over me.

Over the years, I have learned that my initial assumptions—that he was authentic, original, and fundamentally good-hearted—were wrong. When I look back, I wonder how much of my relationship with Jessie was based on this misperception, on my desire for him to be what he was not. Though who needs their art to be true, really? Who needs their art to be the kind of guy who would help you move, who might pick you up from a bar if you'd had too much and got kicked out, who might loan you some money or give you the benefit of the doubt? Who might expect their art to save them from a bullet, stand up for them at their wedding, answer the phone when no one else will? I'd argue none of us deserve that from our art. None of us have earned that.

THE RE-EMERGENCE OF STEPHEN

She was in the bathroom when she found out, on the toilet, her pants and underwear still around her ankles. With Stephen in the hospital, she answered every call, no matter the time of day, no matter what the call interrupted. Though it was an audio call and not a video call, she nodded her head while the woman on the phone told her the news: Stephen was dead.

She'd been visiting him at the hospital every day since the accident, taking the red line out to Rush to check on him, to look at his still body connected to things to which it should not have been connected—a bouquet of plastic, the body's plumbing synthetic and remade around him like some crass tableau. She would wonder what he might say when he woke up, how frustrated he'd be that he wouldn't be able to play his guitar with a broken hand. The cost of recovery, of lost work time. All of that loomed while she watched the machines breathe for him, his eyelashes quiver like they might open, and then not.

Once he died, the people she worked with looked at her through the half-peeled fruit of their eyeballs. They knew what had happened, and she knew they knew. They pitied her. They would happen upon her in the break room, the way you might a road closed sign on a familiar street; their progress arrested, looking for an escape, stupefied. Bianca exposed them with her loss. Revealing them for the scared children that they were, revealing how rudimentary their skill set was for dealing with the things that were real, things that were inevitable.

Her grief gave her a special kind of freedom. Even her superiors deferred to her bereavement, the hierarchy of the company no longer relevant in the face of the new fraternity of which Bianca was a part. Even when she gave up on the coffee altogether and started filling her travel cup with nothing but whiskey, no one said anything. What could they say?

Most people assumed she and Stephen had been married. She had a ring after all. Not a diamond, but it was a ring. He had bought it for her after one of their fights. She thought he was going to leave for good that time. He grabbed his guitar's amplifier and stomped out the door of their apartment. She was surprised when he returned, having sold the amp and bought the ring with the little orange stone in it. They didn't say it, but they knew it meant they were together for the foreseeable.

"If we can't afford to do a big wedding with a band and dancing and all that, then I don't even want to do it," she'd told him post-coital, post-ring, pre-accident.

He agreed that they couldn't afford a wedding, and they instead made a down payment on a little house with bad water pressure. The real estate agent was surprised that they wanted the place, even advised against it. "If you were my kids . . . " she'd said.

They bought it anyway because of where it was situated—equidistant from the towering skyscrapers of the big city and the sprawling estates of the wealthy suburbs. They tried to focus on what they had, rather than what they wanted, who they were rather than who they dreamed they might become.

It was Stephen's idea to go out on the night of the accident, seeing some band Bianca had never heard of play in some venue only he knew about, a whisper network hipping him to the performance. She hadn't wanted to go, but Stephen insisted.

Afterward they drove around the city with nowhere to go while he drunkenly told her about the band they had just seen. Bianca stared at the side of his pretty face, his long hair tied back—she'd always wanted a boyfriend with long hair and now, look, she had one. She wasn't even looking out the windshield when he hit the car while blowing through a red light. Bianca didn't have a scratch on her. Just a sore neck, a sense of profound loneliness the likes of which she'd never felt, and a complete inability to sleep ever after.

Some people from work gave her a sympathy card, and a few people from her department went to the funeral. That was the most embarrassing part of it all. The people who showed up and learned that his body had been cremated already, the casket in the church empty, the whole thing some kind of sham. But it was her sham. The closest thing they'd ever have to a wedding. Even his parents lurked near the back like it had more to do with her than with them. They had never understood him, after all.

And so she'd tried to move forward, drinking and grieving and taking advantage of the situation until she could hide her grief no more. It had become like a pox. Swelling the cells of her, hanging off her like the shutters from an abandoned house.

She knew about the resurrection places. Everyone did. The news would report on places that were shut down. Fringe groups would testify before Congress on the need to legalize the practice, to no avail. Late-night talk show hosts would joke, "If your resurrection lasts longer than four hours, see a doctor . . . "

There were advertisements on internet message boards and rumors of places where one might receive the service, but Bianca worried it was all some kind of trap. That she might call and they would locate her, or she might arrive at an advised location and men with guns would be there waiting for her. It had been illegal for a long time. Anything like that, anything that seemed to upend the natural order of things, was always illegal. How could war be fought anymore if you could bring someone back? And who would be economically responsible for bringing back those dead? The winners or the losers? Plus, the Christians hated it. "Who but God should decide who might be brought back from the dead?" they seemed to be saying.

Bianca wanted to receive the number from someone who could assure her it was real, assure her it was someone with the ability to do what they said, what she needed them to do, to rescue her from her circumstance. But she didn't know anyone like that. That's what she had Stephen for. That's why she needed to get him back.

After Stephen died she couldn't afford their house anymore, and she had to move into a four-bedroom with three other women, all of whom were gentrifying a Hispanic neighborhood, working downtown, wearing blouses, and trying to make it as singers and painters and actresses in their free time. One of them was pregnant. One had a drug problem, and the other one told Bianca about Garret.

"I knew a guy who used one of those resurrection places once," she told Bianca. Bianca was pretty sure the only reason the roommate wanted to help her was so Bianca would move out and the roommate's cousin could move in. Bianca didn't care. She wanted to leave anyway. She didn't know who would even want to move into a place like that, always too cold in the winter and too hot in the summer, the toilets and sinks not working, seeming to regurgitate black bile up from the center of the earth.

"What did he tell you about it?" Bianca asked the roommate, taking the bait.

"He got his son back. That's all I know."

The roommate used to work with Garret at an office building downtown. She said that Garret hadn't been secretive about the fact that he'd resurrected his son, implying that he should have been.

"He seemed proud of it a little. He didn't seem to need to justify it, intellectualize it. He'd just get all weepy and look past whoever he was talking to. That's what turned everyone off about him. How candid he was about the whole deal."

And certainly no one wanted to meet the child. Garret wanted to bring him to work with him. His pride and joy. More proud of the boy than the first time he'd made him.

No one could trust the resurrected boy. No one could be sure he'd been brought back the same. Who knows what he'd seen on the other side of things. And what did it mean about them that they hadn't brought back folks they'd lost?

"He doesn't even remember being dead," Garret insisted. "He hardly knows he was resurrected."

But no one cared.

There was something abnormal about it, they were sure, and so he'd become ostracized and alienated there, and one day, according to the roommate, he'd just stopped coming to work. Bianca didn't like the way the roommate talked about the guy. Like the guy wasn't playing by some set of arbitrary rules.

"We pitied him when it happened, more so when he got the kid back than when he had lost him. When he reversed the natural order for his own selfish aims."

"Can you blame him?"

"It just seems unnatural, is all. But it's totally fine if you want to do it." She shrugged at the end as if it didn't matter. As if Stephen didn't matter.

The roommate had heroically (or selfishly, depending on how you look at it and what you believe about the roommate) stolen the guy's contact info from the HR guy's office. They called him—both women putting an ear to the phone and listening for the resurrected boy in the background, but never hearing him—and they found out where the resurrections were done.

No one ever went to the strip mall anymore. The place was forgotten by all but the few employees necessary to maintain the massage place, the Play it Again Vintage

Record Store, and the restaurant where all the waitresses wore bathing suits. A yoga studio with hand-printed signs sat defiant on the corner. The windows of the remaining stores as cracked as the blacktop of the parking lot. None of the places could be believed. Each store a secret being kept.

Bianca sat in the passenger seat of the roommate's car in the parking lot in front of the Wood Wholesale Warehouse, where Garret had told them the resurrections were performed. Her coffee was bitter with whiskey, biting her lips and filling her behind the eyes with woozy. It was the middle of the day, but the roommate didn't seem to have anywhere to be, and Bianca had stopped showing up for anything.

It didn't seem like a run-down storefront could produce Stephen, grab him from wherever he was. She felt like this was some trick, like the roommate and the internet and the strip mall were in on it together. This was why she needed Stephen back. He always knew things that no one else knew. He probably would have known all about the wood wholesale place. Known that it was a front for another kind of business. Known that their real business was in resurrecting the dead.

"Who sells lumber in a strip mall?" he would have said.

"It's not a lumber place. They sell flooring."

"Then why do they call it Wood Wholesale Warehouse?"

"I think it's important to have alliteration when you name a business."

"Plus, it's not even a warehouse. It's a tiny little store in a strip mall."

"And that's how you know it's a resurrection place?"

"It's a perfect front. It's a place no one would ever go in. They don't even have a working website I don't think."

He always knew about stuff like that. Stuff that was happening just beyond the curtain. Where to get great tapas. Who the bands were that no one even knew about yet. Which strip malls had secret resurrection places. He was no one's fool. He never took anything at face value. Who knows how the two of them ended up together.

She sat in the parking lot in the roommate's car, looking at the Wood Wholesale Warehouse that didn't sell wood wholesale and wasn't a warehouse, and she tried to remember her relationship with Stephen. She tried to figure out exactly how she felt about him. All she could recall after he died was the fights. She wondered if that was what made her want him back so bad. To make up for all the turmoil. But despite the fights—the time she had thrown a porcelain gravy boat at him and barely missed, the time he had called her a fat cunt, the time the neighbors had called the cops on their screaming—there was a thing vital and necessary. Something she had gotten used to having. She thought about who she might become without the relationship and couldn't imagine who that might be.

Bianca took a swig of whiskey from her coffee tumbler and stared unblinking at the place. You were supposed to go in there, into the Wood Wholesale Warehouse—the warehouse understood to be somewhere else, somewhere far away where the wood could be secured and fetched as necessary—and say the proper phrases, and a lady would come out to size you up and try to figure out if you were from the FBI. If she got a whiff, you were out of luck. Properly executing the phrases was your only chance, like some kind of spell you were trying to cast.

"I'm interested in some wood. From the dogwood tree," Bianca said to the girl behind the counter. A teen. She looked unblemished, plastic, and new. Without even bothering to do her hair or put on makeup, she was beautiful. She looked so young she hadn't even had time to get fat. That's how young people look to adults. She looked up at Bianca, like what she'd said was funny.

"Who told you to come?" she asked.

"I'm not supposed to say," Bianca said. The girl nodded, solemn once she'd said that.

"Who is the expired party?"

"It was my husband," she said, deciding they weren't beholden to the laws of man anymore, and so calling him her husband was more true. "Stephen."

"When did the Expiry occur?"

"It wasn't that long ago," she said, realizing how recent it all had been. Six weeks earlier everything had been normal. They'd been arguing over who used more of their data plan, she on her weeping calls to her mother or he on his strange pornography.

"Did you attempt to self–induce resurrection?"

"Should I have?"

"And you have the remains?"

Bianca nodded.

"Do you know what it costs?" the girl asked.

Bianca shook her head.

"It costs everything," the girl said, suddenly seeming older, suddenly looking into Bianca's eyes, suddenly not looking away, suddenly knowing.

The teen turned away and walked into the back of the store. Bianca heard her talk to someone, and then she returned. She told her to call back when she had done what needed to be done. Bianca knew what that meant. She knew it meant to call when she had given everything up.

She sat in her little bedroom in the four-bedroom apartment with the cremains on a table like they weren't him, like the ashes in a box on the table actually belonged in a box on a table. She wondered if there was enough of him in there. If all of him would come back, if he'd be shorter, or missing toes, or not remember her. She wanted to know what would be different.

She feared he would not be like himself. Like the resurrected Stephen would be a scion rather than the man she knew. She wondered if he might inherit traits from elsewhere; the cremains of others scraped from the cremation chamber into the receptacle, the past weighing upon her present, leaving her with problems for which she had no solutions. She worried about new diseases and illnesses, new proclivities. What would she do if he arrived wanting things she could not provide for him or if he wanted to give her things she did not want?

Would things be the same without the house, without the car, without the ring? She wondered if the procedure would bring them together or pull them apart. There was a rumor that her grandmother had brought her own mother back, Bianca's Great-Grandma Perkins. They had been so close before Great-Grandma Perkins caught the Spanish flu, but after she came back, they grew apart. Something came between them, some deep resentment. That was the rumor, anyway. Bianca didn't know if she believed it, and now that they were both dead for good, no one had bothered to bring either of them back to ask about it.

It was usually couples who did it. It was usually the ache of love that ruined everything. The necking in the backseat couples, those living lives so charmed that they couldn't imagine things not going their way; the wild and reckless, the privileged and careless.

There was a reason it was all legislated out of existence. What the resurrections left were people too confused by their circumstances to do anything productive. Just monkeys with bad breath and stinky buttholes, Stephen used to say. She used to roll her eyes when he said stuff like that, but she had come to miss his aphorisms. He talked about people like they were just bumbling around, chewing on a branch that was holding them up, destined to fall to the ground and get splatted.

She got to work getting rid of everything. Stephen had managed to total the car when he'd died, and the house was already gone. She sold Stephen's electric guitar, the one she'd been protecting for that moment when he returned; she cashed in a barely-contributed-to 403(b) plan from her old work; she brought her clothes to the consignment shop she had always been nervous to enter. She put all her things back from whence they'd come, remaking the world as it once was, and she threw up every morning into the backed-up sinks and toilets, hoping to leave it all behind once Stephen returned.

The last thing to sell was her ring. She looked at it while she spoke to the buyer on the phone. He was giving her the same amount Stephen had gotten it for, which was a miracle since she and Stephen had always thought that it was almost worthless, the little stone wrapped in tarnished silver. She remembered when the stone had broken off and she cried as she searched the cushions of that red couch for the little orange pebble. The buyer showed up promptly at the agreed-upon time with a little blue envelope full of money. There was more in there, she could see.

"You sure carry a lot of money around," she said.

"I thought you might change your mind," he confessed and handed the agreed-upon amount out to her. She looked down at the ring. He held the money out, expectant and smiling. The look on his face reminded her of a man she had once seen on a train who had grabbed the cellphone of an unsuspecting passenger and run anxious and wild through the closing doors at the Cicero stop. She asked the ring man to leave. He tried to give her the rest of the money in the envelope, but she turned him down. He became angry and shouted insults at her. She closed the door on him, feeling deep down that it was something Stephen would have done.

She showed up at the facility at night. She found a door open in the alley behind the store. It was like the incision of a laparotomy, the skin peeled back from the abdomen, lurid and revelatory.

"Are you ready?" a woman asked. Bianca recognized that this was the woman who performed the procedures. She wore a mask over her face and a scarf around her neck. She had medical scrubs over her clothes. Bianca wanted to see her face, but all she could see were her hazel eyes, the blue eye shadow she wore thick like a ribbon stretched low across her lids and the sides of her head.

"I don't know," Bianca said. She held the box with his ashes in her hand.

The woman in the mask took the box from her hand and placed it on the table.

"Did you bring me everything?" the woman asked, the stripe of blue widening as she asked the question.

"I lost the house and the car before I even came here," Bianca said.

"Was that all?" the woman asked, as if Bianca's everything was smaller than everyone else's everything.

"I brought you all my money."

"Did you bring me your life from before?"

Bianca tried to understand the riddle.

"I just want it to go back to the way it was."

"It will never be the same," the woman explained.

Bianca nodded her head, knowing that it was true. She had hoped the woman would console her and assure her everything would be okay, but she knew that was not true. No matter how often Bianca would say it to herself or how often she'd be told, she knew it was not true.

The woman in the medical scrubs used a curette to separate the ashes from the sides of the box, organizing Stephen's residue into some sort of manageable shape. Bianca did not understand what the woman was doing, and she tried not to watch, unsure if Stephen could feel it, unsure where his life began and where it ended.

The woman started the procedure, turning on a machine with tubes and dials, cords and wires just like the ones that had been connected to Stephen when he'd been in the hospital. Water pumped through the machine. A bag of clear fluid hung from a lamp and mixed with the water from the hose that came from the sink.

It looked like the pneumatic tube Bianca's mother used to use at the bank. As a child Bianca always wanted to know where those capsules went. Now she knew. They went to heaven to fetch the souls of the deceased to bring them back to earth so they might live again.

While the machine started up, the woman wouldn't look at Bianca. She remained focused on flipping switches, checking monitors, writing things down on a clipboard.

"What are you writing?" Bianca wanted to know.

The teenager from the store came into the room, and now her eyes were painted blue the same way the mask-wearing woman's were. The teen asked a question of the woman that Bianca didn't understand. The woman responded to her question but not Bianca's.

When the machine had been whirring and belching for some time, the box with Stephen's ashes finally began to rumble. It clattered on the table, and the top flipped over. A hand emerged and gripped the side, the fingers like birds lined up on a fallen log. Bianca squinted to try to see if it was his hand. She couldn't tell. She looked for the ring he wore, the one she'd traded her skis for, but then remembered they'd had to cut his fingers off for it, had given it to her with his other effects. It was part of her everything that she'd given up. Everything except her own ring, of course. The ring, she suspected, held some special value that the man who'd come to the apartment had known about and had tried to swindle from her. She'd put the ring on a necklace and hung it around her neck so she could keep it near her without it being seen. As Stephen emerged, Bianca resisted the urge to grab for the ring, worried the woman performing the operation would discover that she had failed to give up this ring, this everything. She should have thrown it down the drain, she realized, but it was too late.

The hand came out, and the arm wrapped itself around the edge of the table. It was covered in dust and ash. Out came a head, the grey ashes caking the face, the dust from the long hair filling the room. Bianca crouched. She couldn't imagine how a man the size of Stephen could emerge from such a small box. But he was. He was emerging, screaming. He was returning to her. It was his hand, his arm, his face, his hair.

The woman did not seem surprised. The teen from the store peeked her head in once more, her eyeshadow like flags staked on taken hills. She looked around, nodded, and then retreated again, still nonplussed at the re-emergence of Stephen.

He pulled himself from the small box, no bigger than a shoe box. He was nude. His grunting steady and primitive.

"Should I hug him?" she asked the woman, like the woman had authority over them in that place. Like she might know how to soothe someone who'd gone through what Stephen had been through.

The woman didn't answer.

Stephen shook his body, the caked grey falling to the ground.

He wrapped a sheet around himself, and Bianca followed him as he ran out into the night. Bianca wasn't sure he even recognized her, but somehow he knew he should run. She caught up to him and corralled him. He looked into her face, and though there was no recollection in his expression, she could tell he was ready for direction. She guided him into her mother's car, borrowed under false pretenses, the roommate long since having been abandoned once she'd given Bianca what she wanted.

Bianca had him back, all long-haired, stubble-faced scruff of him.

"I saved your ring," she said, holding it up to him from the chain around her neck.

"That's not mine," he told her.

They returned to Bianca's new apartment. He had regained his balance, his shame, and his appetite.

"I can make you something to eat," she said, heading for the cabinets, looking for anything good, remembering that she'd only eaten minute rice and Cheez-Its for weeks; remembering that anything else had been impossible to keep down; remembering that the roommates kept most of their food in their own rooms, the distrust for one another as much an accepted reality as the light bill.

"Where are we?" he asked.

"This is where we live now," she said. "I had to sell the house."

He nodded, not remembering the house, but understanding it was lost because of him.

"And the car is gone too?" he asked.

"And the car is gone too."

They decided to leave town, to get new jobs somewhere where no one would know them. Where they wouldn't have to remember all their favorite spots to eat and shop and get their hair cut. Where they wouldn't know themselves.

It turned out the ring was special. Bianca had been right not to sell it to the strange, nervous man who'd tried to give her what Stephen had paid for it. It wasn't made of a common stone but a much rarer stone often mistaken for a near-worthless one. They were rich, more or less, and when they sold the ring for its actual value they were able to buy a house worth more than their original house. And in an unprecedented move, Bianca decided to resell the house to try to make a profit. To everyone's surprise, especially hers, she was able to do so. She felt silly for thinking that she was somehow cursed for not selling the ring. She had everything she wanted. Stephen was back with his long hair, they had experienced a financial boon, and they were starting over.

They also didn't fight anymore, but how could they? How could he blame her for anything when she had traded everything to bring him back? Almost everything. They made themselves so busy that they hardly ever saw each other. His new job was like his other job except more complicated. Her job was like her old one except more stressful. They didn't see bands anymore. He didn't buy his guitar back, music having become an outfit they no longer wore, like the wallet chains and boot-cut jeans modeled in old pictures. He cut his hair, his perfect hair, the hair that had been reborn along with him. It seemed he had done it just to spite her. The only thing he had, and he cut most of it off the same way she had given up everything. Mostly everything.

The only time he was nice to her was when he'd ask her about the resurrection place.

"How did you find out about it?" he wanted to know after he kissed the side of her head. "Where even was it?" he asked since he couldn't remember anything except the pain of rebirth and the combination he had to put into the keypad to get into their new house.

One night she woke to find him sitting cross-legged

on their bed, staring at her.

"What are you looking at?" she asked, wondering if she was still in a dream. "You look like you are going to murder me."

"I want to know where the place is. The place where they brought me back." His face was not his own, just like she'd feared. Nothing was the same as it had been, just like the precocious little shit at the Wood Wholesale Warehouse had said.

In their new car, she drove them to the town where they used to live. She always drove because she didn't trust him behind the wheel any longer. He looked around like it was the first time he'd ever seen anything. He looked like a child on his way to an amusement park, dumb grin stuck on his face.

Bianca parked the car in the lot in front of the Wood Wholesale Warehouse.

"Is this it?" he asked, squinting into the dark, the windows a face slack and dispassionate. He tried to read the signs of the stores in the strip mall, the buildings that had all been something else before: a big box sporting goods store made into a pet shop, a cellphone store remade as a mattress store, a Chinese food place posing as a shoe-repair place. Even the blacktop was repurposed from bicycle tires.

She saw him reach into his pocket, and she was sure that this was it. This was the moment he would kill her, produce a weapon, and use it to interrupt her life. She'd brought a hammer with them on the trip to their old town, one she'd been sleeping with, carrying with her in case things went wrong with Stephen, in case he'd come back from the other side the same way he'd always been.

She thought she was ready to use it, but when he reached into his pocket for what she thought was a gun or a blade, she hesitated, wondering what he might do, what it might be like to be dead and come back. She wondered how that might change things. She gripped the rubber handle of the hammer.

But he didn't pull a weapon from his pocket. He pulled out the ring. He'd bought it back at more-than-full price from whomever they'd sold it to, their success allowing such an extravagant purchase. He hadn't wanted to kill her. He'd made her bring them back to the strip mall because he wanted to see what had made him, the source of his new existence.

She understood the impulse.

When the hammer connected with his skull, it split like it was a weeping boil. She continued to hit him until he stopped moving. He screamed while she hit him. Dazed and his forehead turning purple and black with welts.

Once he was dead the woman who'd performed the operation and the arrogant teenager approached the car. The woman who'd done the procedure, the one with the blue eye shadow, didn't wear a mask and Bianca could see her face. She didn't look concerned or surprised about being called into service once again.

"Unbuckle his seat belt," the woman said, and the teenager opened his door, tugging at the legs of the body, trying to get them out of the car.

It took them a minute, but they were able to dislodge the corpse. The teenager slipped her arms underneath the armpits and walked backwards towards the Wood Wholesale Warehouse, the feet of the body scribbling static into the grey warp of the parking lot.

The woman with the blue eye makeup reached into the car and pulled the keys from the ignition like they were hers all along.

"Are you coming in?" the woman asked.

Bianca shook her head, and the woman did not try to change her mind.

"Did you bring everything this time?" the woman asked.

Bianca slipped an envelope into the woman's hand. Just like the last time, the envelope was filled with magic scripts, words and spells that would give over ownership of all Bianca's worldly possessions. Before the woman could ask about it, Bianca picked up the ring that had fallen into the footwell of the car, the ember of the orange stone seeming to change color in the parking lot lights. Bianca stared into the bright of the gem, knowing she had to hand it over.

YOU WOULD UNDERSTAND WHY I'M LIKE THIS IF YOU WERE THE EXACT SAME PERSON AS ME

Neither of them could remember whose idea it was to read the book. The only book in the house that they had two copies of. It was as if the books were placed there with some kind of intention. It took them a while to read it. He read the first hundred pages in a single evening, and she didn't get started for another week. He put the book down and let himself be distracted by other things, but she continued and read a few pages each day. She found herself savoring it, and when she finished, she urged him to complete it because she found it so moving, so beautiful, so sad.

"You thought it was beautiful?" he asked, raising his eyebrow in that way he did that was almost as if to say: *What if I raised my eyebrow like this, wouldn't it be terribly dismissive and superior?* and yet even with the self-awareness of the gesture, it still came off as terribly dismissive and superior, perhaps more so than if he'd been oblivious. "And moving? Are you sure you don't mean gauzy and melodramatic? Rendered with purple prose and a heavy hand?"

"You are being so prescriptive."

"I am not. I am merely meeting the book on its own terms and pointing out the ways in which it fails."

"You'd understand if you were in my shoes."

"Come on. It's not like that. It's not like I can't understand this book just because it was written by someone who doesn't look like me. I like all kinds of books. I love Toni Morrison, for example."

"Everyone loves her. That doesn't count."

"I'm just saying I am able to like books by queer women of color. I just don't like this one."

"Toni Morrison wasn't gay."

"I didn't say gay. I said queer."

"I'm not sure you're allowed to say that word."

"Now who is being prescriptive?"

"You'd understand why this book is so great if you could see where I'm coming from."

Mitch realized in a sudden, humiliating moment that Allison was right. And in a rare foray into honesty, both with his wife and with himself, he told her as much. When she came home from work the next day, he was wearing her underwear.

"Fuck me," he said. "Fuck me like I fuck you."

"Do you think that is what will make you understand the book?"

"Do it."

And she tried, but to no avail.

So, he found someone who could oblige. Near enough.

First, a truck driver named Jerry who smelled like onions. Then Mitch's best friend. Finally, a prostitute who looked good until he smiled and revealed his tiny little teeth, tiny like the tiny pebbles that pile up at the bottom of a fish tank.

Mitch noticed Allison going from combative to cordial, always a sign of the end of things. She spent a lot of time on the phone and met with someone who Mitch assumed was a lover. Mitch got drunk in a bar and got himself into a circumstance that was dangerous and ill-advised, but still he did not understand the book. He knew the only way to do it would be to go back to the beginning and live Allison's life from infancy. And so he did.

Her childhood was beautiful to him. For the most part. Except for that time with Brooks Shelley in the tub when no one else was looking. And that time she got 12 stitches because her sister accidentally stabbed her in the head with a TV antenna. But even that was beautiful because Mitch knew she would survive it, and it was nice to see Mia and Sam still together and Brandi still alive and feeling guilty for hurting Allison. It was beautiful to look up and see everyone looking down with love, those eyes aimed sympathetically at Mitch as he experienced Allison's life.

There were those tough high school years, of course, and those years where she was pretending to be going to college when she was actually waitressing and squandering all her money on booze, but those had their high points as well. Mitch tried to enjoy them where he could, the way any young person enjoys their misspent youth. When things became too difficult, too sad, too humiliating, he would remind himself that it wasn't he who was feeling these things, but Allison. Though that could sometimes make it worse.

It was hard for Mitch to have to quit Allison's job at her father's company. Sam had given her the job after she'd been fired from the restaurant, and the time when Allison had that job was a good time, a time of calm and eating dinner with her dad and stepmom a couple times a week, and a time of trying to get herself together even though she was still drinking. But Mitch knew Allison had quit the job, and so he would have to quit the job even though he knew that doing so would eventually turn out to be a bad idea for her. Allison didn't know it at the time, but there wouldn't be a way to understand the book if he didn't make all the mistakes as her that she had made.

And there was being attacked in the parking lot, of course, and that turned out to be the most awful even though he knew it was coming. Especially because he knew it was coming.

Meeting himself turned out to not be as cinematic as he had expected. From Allison's perspective, Mitch could see that he was a bit pompous. A bit miserable and needy, it turned out. More than he'd thought. More than he'd realized.

By the time he got to read the book as her, with all of her experiences, with her perspective whittled by the blade of her triumphs and pains, he'd almost forgotten what he'd been doing. It had been 34 years, after all. But when he came across the book as Allison it seemed like the most natural thing in the world. It was like a tongue slipping into a groove.

There were the books placed neatly on a shelf, identical copies, though one was slightly discolored. They looked like an artifact from childhood, like they belonged to his parents, like they were something he was not supposed to touch but was going to anyway. Mitch, coming to the book with Allison's experiences layered on top of his own like long-sleeve shirts in late fall, read it at first with interest, then hungrily. And then with dread that the end was near. He cried at moments when he wasn't sure he was supposed to cry, and he laughed when the two side characters wound up together for the first time, and he felt sick to his stomach when news of the father reached the protagonist. It was like the book knew him, knew what he wanted, what he expected, and then used that to manipulate him. It was like someone had pulled a sheet away from him that he'd been using to cover his naked body. And rather than being ashamed he found himself stimulated by being naked. He felt wrung out and cold but glad of it. Seen.

Mitch, who was now Allison, hardly even cared that her husband didn't seem to like or understand the book; she could hardly muster the energy to argue with him. Having completed the book, Allison called the original Allison to let her know that she'd been right all along. Allison, the original Allison, was retired by this point and lived alone, it having taken Mitch 34 years to get to the point where she could read the book and understand it. The two women sat down for dinner.

"How is he?" the elder Allison asked. "Still full of anger and malice?"

"It's not malice," Allison, who used to be Mitch, said to her older self, before realizing Mitch could be malicious sometimes. He could be mean and cruel.

"When I was him I didn't know I was being cruel. I was mostly sad."

The elder Allison nodded, knowing it to be true. The younger Allison, who did not usually feel young but did so in this circumstance, looked upon her older self with wonder and admiration but also dread.

They talked for a long time without mentioning any

incarnation of Mitch again. The elder Allison offered insight but did not reveal too much, and the younger Allison, being in closer proximity to the past, reminded her older self of wonderful things that had happened to them both, things of which the elder Allison was glad to be reminded. The two spoke like strangers who had both attended the same school unbeknownst to one another at the time, two people who knew all the same people, who had coincidentally been to all the same places. Allison the younger, the Allison who used to be Mitch, felt stunned and new but also weary and resigned to the knowledge that it had always been this way.

They talked about the divorce, leaving home, getting tapped; they talked dry-mouthed into the color swatch of the night—the air wetter than it was black. They talked about the house their dad sold after the divorce and all that went with it, and they admitted to each other how much it all meant. The older Allison was relieved to finally have someone to tell, and the younger was relieved to hear it all put into words that way. She felt exculpated somehow. And humid. Cross.

The newer Allison returned to her husband, who was aloof and malicious but sometimes kind and tender. He did not understand the book, could not love it like she did, and Allison learned to accept that and to love other things that he loved. He never even bothered to finish it before leaving her, and Allison learned to accept that as well. Once he was gone, she thought back on her life like it was a life lived by someone else, and she waited until she would be the elder Allison and she would receive a phone call from her younger self who used to be her husband, and she wondered what that might be like.

THE PARTS OF A SHADOW

> "Thus Children are ever ready, when novelty knocks, to desert their dearest ones . . . and so it will go on, so long as children are gay and innocent and heartless."
>
> —J. M. Barrie, *Peter Pan* (1911)

As I tracked Peter through the city, exactly 22 paces behind, I kept my eyes peeled for attacks from King Ninja Fairy and his machines. I made sure to keep silent, holding my breath as I pursued, only exhaling when a car passed by, the exhaust smelling like a rotten egg split open. The smells of The World were amazing and beautiful—the hot stink coming from the sewers; the bite on the back of my tongue from the rust of half-completed buildings; the accumulated smell of bodies, their scent amplified by the heat.

I had been on Peter's tail all day. I'd spotted him by the zoo, followed him past the stadium, and lost track of him by the station. He should have been easy to find again. He was just a kid, after all, and even though he was technically born before me, I was a whole year older than him. Plus, he had never seen a city before, so he should have stuck out like a crocus in a patch of crabgrass.

Stumbling from street to street, the umbra of his shadow slipping over everything.

The Parts of a Shadow

There are three distinct parts of a shadow, you see; the umbra, the penumbra, and the antumbra. You're a little surprised that I know all those big words, aren't you? Well, I do. These big Wikipedia words are what doctors and geniuses use to describe shadows cast by heavenly bodies, but they can also be used to describe levels of darkness. What is left after a light source encroaches upon an object, as they say.

The umbra is the super-dark inside part of a shadow, especially the area on the earth or moon experiencing the total phase of an eclipse. The umbra is the real deal. The good stuff. That hardcore, black-as-night type of shadow. It's the stuff people make shadow puppets out of and long for on a hot day. It's what Peter lost when he crawled into Wendy's room that night everyone talks about constantly, as if that was the only thing Peter ever did and she was the only person he ever met. I'm not jealous. I'm just saying. (I've met her, by the way. In case you were wondering. She's fine. A little bit of a know-it-all, but fine.)

Since Peter's shadow was made up of the darkest of dark, I should have been able to keep track of it. I had lost him and his shadow at the Washington stop though, near where you could see the water tower through the forest of tall buildings. He looked like he wasn't going to get off, but then at the last moment he changed his mind and slipped through the doors, his shadow sliding out the other exit to meet him on the sidewalk. I should have known

Peter was going to do that. After all, I knew him better than anyone. By the time Stegosaurus and I got to the next stop, got off the bus and hopped onto one that would take us back to Washington, Peter and his shadow both were gone. The bus shelter was still and empty, the white paint of the posts translucent from the cold.

I'd lost him to the city. He was out there somewhere wearing those dumb clothes the house parents from his group home had given him—a shirt that spilled off him like loose shingles cascading off an old roof, jeans that were so tight that I could see his lucky thimble tucked into the pocket. Sometimes he would wear it on a chain around his neck, dangling it in the space between his clavicles. I would watch it, wanting it, hypnotized by it as it tumbled back and forth on his chest. Sometimes the light would catch it, and it would gleam like a big, dumb moon in the night. I would imagine hanging onto the necklace as he leapt over things in The World and dodged around stray animals, as if the chain were the rope of a life preserver keeping me from going under. But usually, like I said before, he just kept it in his pocket.

What people from Neverland call The World:

- The Always World
- The Sometimes World
- The World of Adults
- The World-world
- The City-World
- The Grown-Up World
- The Place to the North
- The World

The day we'd been returned to The World, it was Halloween and everyone was dressed like Pirates and Peters and shivering to look like Tink, the costumes piled up on the men doing a poor job covering up the pink of their desire. The women hardly wore anything at all. None of them actually looked like Pirates, or Peter, or Tink. Not really. They were drunk and trying to be merry, but instead were crying and throwing up in the street.

We don't have Halloween in The Never because we don't have October. It is never brown and dead. It skips right from the wrinkled greens and golds of September to the snowmen and plum pudding of December. It is only ever California or Antarctica. And sometimes it rains.

No one is Christian either, but everyone celebrates Christmas. Neverland is the late 1980s, the lurid colors of those movies and television shows, the dim naiveté of D.A.R.E. programs and school-sponsored dental exams. No one in The Never needs to dress up for Halloween to escape because who would want to escape Neverland? They have already escaped. No one has to "cut loose" by pretending to be a monster or a swordsman because we are monsters, we are swordsmen every day.

What do the People in Neverland Call People From The World?

- Normals
- Normies
- Growns
- Groans
- Northerners

Peter had an altogether different experience with his social worker than I had with mine. He had a man, first of all, who wore a tie and a crisp yellow shirt and who walked on long, storky legs that made him look not just like a Groan, but like an adult. He had been looking for Peter for weeks, having kept a daily slot in his calendar open like a window meant for a lost puppy to return through. The social worker man finally found Peter playing touch football in a nearby parking lot and was able to coax him back to his office. Peter only went with the social worker that day because he wanted to play some mischief, because he was bored and a little curious, and also because his team was losing its game by two touchdowns. When Peter dropped the neon-green foam football and followed the man, his shadow gliding over parked cars and storefronts like the last ice cube sliding from a cup, I stood from where I was hiding and followed them.

I had been to the office a few weeks earlier. I went right after they evacuated Neverland and brought us back to The World. The Never was a place, it turned out. A place to which the laws of space and time didn't quite apply, but it was a place nonetheless. And it was a place with trees, so the Northerners wanted those since they seemed to have cut down all their own trees. So, due to all that, roads inched closer and closer to the heart of The Never, ships took supplies to the island and resources from it, and trucks pressed the earth down, taming it, wearing it out, reminding it that it was dirt.

I learned all this from my social worker.

She spent a lot of time telling me things I didn't really want to know. I am not sure why she did that. It just seemed to make her more unhappy.

My social worker was a woman, as I think I've already mentioned, but she wasn't very much like a mother. She looked swollen, like a foot stuck with prickers, and she wore perfume that I guess was supposed to smell like flowers but didn't smell like any flowers I had ever sniffed. The Groan who was in charge of me told me I was supposed to go see her, and I went even though I had better things to do. Stegosaurus went with me, but I had him wait outside so they wouldn't know he was there, so they couldn't make a record for him too. He slipped around on the outside of the building and tried to get a look in the dirty, oversized windows. I walked into the building and watched the reflection of the lights on the wax floor as they seemed to try to evade me all the way to the door of the social worker's office.

"Everything is different now," she explained, "from the last time you were here."

"Is that so?" I asked her.

"Yes. We've had a black president now, for example. A president of Asian descent. And a woman president too."

"You mean you've never had any of those before?" I asked her, almost curious. She didn't like that.

"I hear you didn't want to come here today," she said. "Well, I didn't want to come here either, you know. I'd love to sit around and do nothing, instead of come here. I'm looking for another job, needless to say."

I didn't know what I was supposed to say to that, and I guess she didn't know what to say either, so she just held up a little shiny object made of glass and plastic, hardly larger than her palm, and she showed me images on it, images that would materialize in the space between us. She showed me all kinds of things on that machine.

Things I didn't really care to see, to be honest.

"I'll bet you wonder how I did that," she said after she put her little object back in her drawer, smiling at all the pictures she had created.

"Not really," I told her. "We have had magic in The Never for a long time."

I'll bet you know how she felt about that.

The day I followed Peter, tagging along as his social worker led him into the brick office building, me several paces behind and Stegosaurus several paces behind me, the woman I talked to wasn't there. She must have been off that day. Or maybe she finally got that other job she wanted. Or maybe she died.

What Peter's Social Worker's Face Looked Like:

- Like a duffel bag stuffed with towels
- Like a saturated napkin
- Like a smaller book being squished by two larger books
- Like a half-eaten sandwich

The man, the man with the face, presented Peter with the proposition of school, something never presented to me, not before Neverland and certainly not when I had met with my own social worker weeks earlier. But that's what the man with the face was pushing. Peter wasn't paying attention though. He was slowly walking around the office, letting his gaze guide him to the corners and tiny pockets of the office that most compelled him. Like a cold hand seeking heat under a blanket, Peter sought out the strange and the colorful in the man's office.

"But I can't read or write," declared Peter, gladly.

"I don't think they care anymore," said the man as he wrote things down on the form in front of him.

"Capital!" cried Peter, happily.

"What are you, eleven? Twelve?" he asked Peter. Peter just shrugged.

While the man poured all his attention into his work, Peter stared at the top of the man's head. His hair looked like a cake, overcooked but beautiful. The man stuck out his tongue as if writing about the boy was performing a difficult task.

"You need to be in school," declared the social worker man, directly contradicting what the woman who spoke with me had said.

"According to your date of birth," my social worker had said, "you are too old to be in school. And if you want a driver's license, you'll have to take the driving test. Not just the written."

I realize now that I should not have told her when I was born. But she asked me my date of birth, and by the way she said it, I could tell she didn't think I would know. Maybe that was why I told her, just so she would be surprised that I knew. But she shouldn't have been surprised if you ask me. What kid doesn't know his own birthday?

When I talked to her, I tried to tell her the truth about what I wanted and what I planned to do since going back to Neverland was out of the question. She didn't want to hear what I had to say about things, though.

"Well, do you have perfect vision?" she asked. "Because a pilot needs to have perfect, or better than perfect vision, so if you want to be a pilot, that is the first thing you need. Did you know that?"

I squinted at her and took note of tiny details on her

face, the dark ridge along her forehead, the way her hair was tugged tight like a hay bale on her head, the mole on her neck. I told her, "I can see you, can't I?"

That made her write something down. Sure enough.

She asked me my name, so I told her, but she didn't like that either.

"Not your nickname," she said. "Your real name."

"That is my real name," I told her. "People really say it and I, for real, say back: *What's up?* Changing it now would just confuse things."

"All the other boys we rescued chose real names."

"They already had real names."

"And you are telling me that you think 'Tootles' and 'Jangles' are real names? Do you think a person can just put a name like 'Slightly' on a job application?"

I didn't know what to say to that because I did think they were real names. As real as hers, anyway. *Deborah.*

After I left the office, I had my new name, a pair of eyeglasses, and a way to draw Social Security checks, but Stegosaurus was gone. He must have gotten bored waiting for me and wandered off or been murdered by pirates. Or gang members. Or the government. I normally wouldn't have cared, but after getting my name changed, I thought it would have been nice to have someone call me by the name I was going by in Neverland. My real name.

What I spent my Social Security check on:

- candy
- ice cream
- a box of cars I haven't played with yet
- comic books (though I guess they call them graphic novels now)

Peter told the social worker man, the man with the face, that he would go to school, but he left the office with no intention of doing so. I had known Peter for too long not to know when he was lying, which was often. Peter kicked over a garbage can in the hall and bumped into a water cooler, spilling the water all over the worn, brown tiles of the government building; the water crept across the floor like a runner stumbling toward a finish line.

None of the other kids waiting to see social workers seemed to notice or care. The boys stood in the hallway, the soles of their sneakers pressed against the wall, their bottom lips holding up their sour faces. The girls, already women, had their tattooed arms folded in defiance. Some were fat from nearly-free, government-backed sugar, while others were too thin to stand up straight, the methamphetamines making their bodies frail and stooped.

Following Peter through the street, it was always dusk, always cool enough to need a jacket but not so cool that it needed to be zipped. When he was hungry, he stole food from the street vendors or from the tables of people who ate on patios and under awnings at ethnic restaurants. They all seemed so charmed by him, they all seemed to relish being robbed.

"That boy is going to be a pilot one day. I can tell just by looking at him."

Things Peter likes to say:

- "Capital!"
- "Don't be so stodgy!"
- "Lads . . . "
- "Passing queer."
- "It is a princely scheme."

- "Am I not a wonder? Oh, I am a wonder."
- "Dunderhead"
- "I will blood him severely."
- "Stow this gab!"
- "You silly ass!!"
- "Screw your courage, man. Screw it to the sticking place!!!"
- "It's Saturday, after all."

That's what he always said whenever he wanted to do something. "Should we play soccer under the moon tonight? It's Saturday, after all." "Should we go skinny dipping in The Cove? It is Saturday, after all." "Should we? Should we? Should we? It's Saturday . . . "

Things Peter Deludes Himself that he Never Does:

- Farts
- Sleeps
- Shoves
- Cries
- Freaks out after he gets water in his nose
- Bleeds

I followed Peter a little bit longer. As it continued to get dark. He walked through the streets and let his curiosity guide him. He lifted up scraps of paper and shreds of clothing, kicking empty bottles into the street to see what sounds they would make, crowing softly to find out who might be annoyed and who might be emboldened by his cry.

Other Parts of a Shadow

I never told you about the other parts of a shadow. You'll want to know about the penumbra. The penumbra is the sort of fuzzy outer region of the shadow. It's not like the umbra. You've seen it. When the sun slides across the sky on some heated evening where the AC is busted, and you stare at the strange, squashed diamond shapes the shutters make on the ceiling, that's the penumbra. That lighter shadow. The lesser one just a few steps behind the real shadow. That's all of us. Peter's penumbra. The dim copies surrounding him, aping him, wishing we could be closer to the center, to what is making the shadow. In Latin, I guess it means "almost shadow," which sounds about right. Who hasn't been someone's penumbra.

I Try to Think About How We All Got Back Here to The World

I am pretty sure it started when we were having a brain fruit fight, throwing them at each other in our underground home like they were snowballs. There was brain fruit everywhere that summer. The strange, bump-afflicted fruit covered the ground, inside and out, like warts grown by the soil. They certainly weren't good for eating. But for throwing? Capital!

We threw the green, stone-like fruits at one another, hiding behind our makeshift furniture and using our covers and sleeping bags as a fort to protect us. One of the sleeping bags was ripped to shreds during the game, of course. Peter stopped his throwing and halted the game to stare us all down with equal measures of sorrow and mean delight in his eyes. He announced that someone would be sleeping outside that night, and it wouldn't be him. There was a long silence before I figured out what to do. I picked one of the brain fruits and threw it at Yusuf. Yusuf was sad-eyed and quiet, his cheeks sagging from his sallow, dusty face. I picked him because I knew he wouldn't fight back.

"Let's oust Yusuf to King Ninja Fairy and his band of evil robots," I had said to the others. To Tootles and Stegosaurus, to Peter and Angel. I can't tell you why I picked Yusuf, except to say that I didn't like him. Not at all. Not that day, anyway.

"Let's leave him locked out so they swing by and pick him up and tie him to a bale of hay and set him on fire," I suggested because I had seen such behavior in an old movie.

"No one likes Yusuf. I don't know why he came to Neverland to begin with," someone said. It might have been me, or it might have been someone else. In the excitement, who could tell?

The lost boys all laughed at the thought of Yusuf alight and screaming, and I thought that even if the Pirates didn't tie him to a hay bale and burn him up, it was a thrilling, a strange, and a horrifying image nonetheless, and it might be exciting to imagine it and then to bring it up again later. Peter loved being thrilled, after all. Everyone does.

Yusuf's shoulders slumped as Angel threw a brain fruit of his own. Though it missed him, the look on Yusuf's face registered as if it had connected. He looked around like he had done something wrong, but he wasn't sure what.

Peter smiled in that way only Peter could. And he waited and he watched while we threw brain fruit at poor Yusuf, who could only duck as we imagined new and more horrible ways for The Pirates or the redskins, the cannibals, or the starting lineup of the 1976 Philadelphia Flyers to come and murder and torture him. Peter laughed and crowed suddenly, smoothing out the tumult like a wave smashing onto a beach.

"Or we could toss you out," he said to me.

How Peter Smiled

- Like a snake digesting
- Like a car full of gasoline
- Like two birds rutting
- Like a monster after its meal
- Like a henchman after a kill
- Like the last of a species, ready to dive from a rock
- Like a spark, leaping loose from a frayed cord

"Wait," I begged. "What about King Ninja Fairy?"

Fingers wrapped tight around my arms like mindless, otherworldly belts tightening around my flesh. They pressed into my skin and shoved me toward the door.

"Cast the carrion overboard," someone said. It might have been Peter, but I couldn't turn my head so I can't be sure.

Yusuf looked stunned that he had been granted a reprieve, that his fate had been reversed, that he might sleep in a warm sleeping bag, with the bodies of all his friends and compatriots surrounding him instead of being thrown out in the cold and/or lashed to a hay bale and burned to death. He put his hands on me too, taking up the mantle of the ouster, just as easily as he had accepted being the ousted.

I tried to set my feet, but I couldn't fight the tide of all those lost boys shoving me out the door. I found myself outside in the dark, and though it was summer that day, I felt the cold of the wind bite down on my bones.

I felt small.

I knew I would be folded back into things the next day,

after I'd crawled into the bushes and gotten crocuses stuck in my hair all night, after they'd found me the next day and all laughed at me for looking foolish. But I didn't want to look foolish, I didn't want to give Yusuf the satisfaction. And I didn't want Peter to laugh at me. So I started walking. Out of spite, I headed North, toward where I knew there were roads and buildings and Groans. A place the lost boys had made a silent pact to avoid because we knew that only civilization could be found there. Being tossed out so unfairly filled me with a higher level of defiance and anti-authoritarianism than usual. A defiance usually reserved for The World and for Groans, but this time directed towards my fellow lost boys and at Peter.

When I got to the blacktop, emerging from the forest with my face smudged with dirt and dark from the night, there were cars running along the road. More cars than I remembered being on that road the last time I had made a trip to the North. Also, there happened to be a gas station that I didn't remember. I could see giant pictures of candy and hot dogs in the window. I was pretty hungry and so I thought I might go in and raid the coins from the "take a penny / leave penny" tray and try to come up with enough money to buy some gum or a donut.

I was never able to pull off the heist, though. A woman who was buying sunglasses and gasoline was able to ascertain with one look that I was a lost boy (or "misfit" as she called me). She wore a sharp blazer, and she wrinkled the skin above her forehead a lot. She could tell I was untethered from my parents and totally free, and I guess she got jealous because she immediately wanted to apprehend me. Being that she was a full-functioning member of The World, she couldn't allow my freedom to continue, and she started asking me questions.

When I told her about Neverland, she sent a S.W.A.T. team in there. Or, I don't know if she sent them herself, but as a result of her meddling, the men with guns were sent into The Never. Can you even believe it, though? A S.W.A.T. team? To go and snatch up Peter? Wouldn't that kind of make you proud if you were such a danger they needed a S.W.A.T. team to come and get you? They were so afraid of him, or at least where we were living, that they needed automatic weapons and canisters of tear gas. And some helicopters too I think, and air support, dogs, and snipers. All of it.

When they closed the door of that white van, Peter and Angel and Yusuf and Tootles were all lined up in there, facing each other like the seeds of a sliced-open kiwi. It made me wonder if it was the last time I would ever see them. Or if it was the last time they would see me, sitting in the car of the woman with the blazer, listening to music, eating a taco-rito from the gas station.

I knew they wouldn't get their hands on Stegosaurus, though. He was too slippery. And he had a weird kind of luck. He was probably shitting outside the fort when the Navy SEALs raided it or off peeping on the mermaids in The Cove. As the woman in the blazer pulled the car out of the gas station parking lot, her headlights pointed at The World, the gravel creaking beneath the tires, I saw Stegosaurus stumble into the street, watching as the cars drove away and I wondered what would happen to him.

The Last Part of a Shadow

The last part of a shadow that you need to know about is the antumbra, and that's easy. That's the one for when you go all the way. That's what you see when the moon is totally overtaken and encircled by the sun. Completely consumed and dwarfed. So much so that when it happens, the moon, Earth's tiny satellite, is just a dot on the hungry sun. It happens to everyone eventually. But, think about it this way: it's the moon that makes the sun's corona seem so thick, like a goddamn golden ring in the sky.

Finally Finding Peter

I couldn't tell if he knew I'd been following or if his whimsy had pulled him in too many new directions for me to follow. It was about the time I noticed Stegosaurus had caught back up with me. He hadn't been murdered by wildcats or barbarians after all. He was trying and failing to hide in a half-full garbage can. He was probably ashamed of leaving his post in front of the social worker's office and was now trying to make up for it. *Well, I'll show him*, I decided.

I snuck onto a bus through the back door and sat in one of the seats in the rear that were turned sideways. No one noticed me, and I watched them twist their faces and try to make their phone calls, try to read their books.

I got off at Washington and then followed the smell of weed smoke. The scent of it wafted side to side like a meandering skunk. I knew Peter would want to follow it to find out what it was.

The Kinds of Villains You Can Find in The Never:

- Pirates
- Buccaneers (which are like pirates but are somehow different, Peter assures us)
- Soldiers

- Ninjas
- Musketeers
- Terrorists
- Martians
- The Government
- People who piss upwind of you
- Guerrillas
- Gorillas
- Apes
- Dinosaurs
- Wildcats
- Redskins
- People who don't bury their shit when they shit
- The pantheon of Greek and Roman Gods
- Gangsters
- Gangstas
- Yer mom
- Principals
- Guys named Chad
- People who fart under the blanket and won't lift it up to let out the smell, which is called a Dutch oven, I guess
- People who say that they are going to do something and make you feel like they are going to do it, but then don't do it and make you feel dumb for thinking they would do it to begin with

I found him on a stoop, clothes all wrinkled and ill-fitting, his smile cracked into a grin, his head thrown back in laughter. He was shorter than his compatriots but commanded them, nonetheless.

I was flattened and embarrassed by the sight of him,

trapped in the antumbra.

"If we meet King Ninja Fairy in open fight, you must leave him to me," Peter told one of the kids on the stoop, one they were calling Peanut. They stood there like they were balanced on top of a volcano or were taking their places on the bridge of a spaceship.

"No problem," Peanut said.

"You got it. That motherfucker is yours," said another. He laughed, but I couldn't tell if he was laughing because he thought the idea of Peter killing King Ninja Fairy was funny or because he was high. The kids had the same look as the kids in the social worker's office, mean, fragile, and coiled.

Peter puffed on the joint, the cherry on the tip glowing magnificently. He was adept, of course, in spite of never having done it before, and the bright red of the fiery cherry was reflected in his beautiful eyes.

He laughed warmly. It enveloped us all.

They finished the joint and emerged from the stoop like a school of fish bursting from a reef, all in a group, with a noise and a color. Peter looked like he was going to pass me, but I saw recognition gleam in his eyes, those eyes like broken glass at the bottom of a pool.

"Hey, Peter," I said to him.

"Hey," he said, stopping at the foot of the steps. He squinted his eyes at me, trying to determine if he knew me, probably a little unsure because of those new, stupid eyeglasses the social worker had given me. I saw his eyes go steady—settle on me like a bird coming to rest on a telephone wire. Eyes so bright, like silverware polished until it made your hand ache.

"You know him?" asked Peanut.

In that moment I hated Peanut. I hated that he would expose Peter like that, embarrass him. But Peter wasn't embarrassed, of course. He just oozed against the stoop, his body fitting between the cracks of the stone.

"Yeah," said Peter, unsteady as a drunk in the morning. "Yeah, I know him."

I smiled, and he laughed. My stomach felt like it had flopped out of me and onto the sidewalk. His laugh convulsed him, grabbed a hold of him. Grabbed a hold of everyone.

Stegosaurus, for a moment, forgot he was hiding under a pizza box on the next stoop over, and I could hear him laughing, too. And it felt good, like it was something that used to happen a lot, something that maybe we took for granted, but that happened no more.

And for a second, I thought that it might be okay. That I could explain it all to Peter, revealing that I too had been evacuated to this city, that Stegosaurus was hiding in a pizza box, and that we shared some special secret knowledge, but I couldn't bring myself to do it. I wanted to explain that it was my fault we were no longer where we loved to be, and I wanted to ask him if he knew what happened to Yusuf. I thought that maybe he might even call me by my name, my real name, slap me on the back, and forgive me. Or even punch me in the gut, just to get it over with.

But I didn't say anything. To be absolved would require me to face his wrath, which wasn't so terrible. Not really. But I couldn't bear to take the blame, to be held accountable for ending the gladness we had felt in The Never, or even the gladness he was feeling with his fellows from the stoop. I resolved to return the next day, but I knew he would not be there. So ephemeral was he that he would never allow himself to form something so rigid and adult-like as a habit.

So, I watched as they all slid from the bottom step of the stoop and spilled onto the sidewalk, Peter and his new fellows, the umbra of his shadow inching across the cement, the penumbras close behind, longing to be closer to the center. And I pitied them, all those fake versions of him trying futilely to keep up, because I knew that it was me who made Peter special. It was me who made him into that goddamn golden ring in the sky. It was my moon that made Peter's sun so special. It had been me all along.

A UNIFIED CONSPIRACY THEORY

When Jack walked into the Nite Owl Diner, I almost didn't recognize him. He was heavier than the last time I had seen him, and his hair was cut short, but he smiled the same way he always had. He had this expectant look on his face, as if the counter, the register, the grill, the worn floors, the uncomfortable booths—all of it were part of some elaborate surprise party set up just for him.

I had been coming to the Nite Owl almost every day because it was the only place I could get my research done. It was nice of my sister to put me up in her apartment and everything, but her television didn't work, which made it difficult to continue looking for the Pattern. I'd tried the electronics store, but they'd gotten wise to me real quick. The only place that had free cable TV was that diner where pretty much no one ever came.

So, even though it had filthy bathrooms and the coffee was so weak it made me sleepy, I would walk down there and spend all day spotting hidden configurations in the programming: Illuminati symbols in commercials, coded language in news stories, secret instructions in talk shows. I also flipped through stacks of magazines and newspapers that I had pilfered from waiting rooms and front porches. Evidence of the Pattern was everywhere, but I was looking for the big one. The smoking gun. The clue that would link it all together. I felt like I was close.

The sound was usually off on the TV, but that actually made it easier to see the symbols buried in the corporate logos and the hand signals they forced the actors to make. When I found something on television that lined up with what I was reading, I would make a note on the page, tear it out, and put it in a pile to be filed when I got back to my sister's place.

I always sat in the same booth, the one right near the TV. The booth was stiff and bothered my back, but pretty much everything bothered my back: the energy from high-tension wires, the chemicals the government streaked across the sky, Democrats. The same waitress and short-order cook would always be there, grinning like they had some special, secret knowledge I didn't. They would look at me and then whisper to each other in a language I was pretty sure was Spanish. I wondered how dumb they would feel if they found out I spoke Spanish and knew every word they were saying. I mean, I don't speak Spanish, but wouldn't it have been great to see the looks on their faces if I whipped out a little *Qué hora es?* They were always trying to get me to buy their terrible food and drink their fluoridated water, but I knew better. I just nursed a cold cup of coffee, rolled my cigarettes, and tried to concentrate on my research.

Then Jack walked in, looking a little tired but still with the appearance of a man who knew he deserved things. I wasn't sure why he'd shown up. Had he traced me here because of all the stuff that had gone down with Esther

Shelton all those years ago? I was worried I would have to tell him I was sleeping on the floor of my sister's studio apartment and still hadn't snuck into Bohemian Grove or kidnapped any of Robert McNamara's grandchildren to prove they had reptilian blood or done any of the other things I had ever talked about doing. Jack smiled at the plump, acned waitress and demanded a booth like it was his damn inheritance or something. Then, pretending he'd only just seen me, he came right over. I stood up. I thought he might hit me, but he just grabbed my hand and shook it without shaking it. We stood there, gripping each other's hands and squinting. I tried to squeeze harder than him. I felt like he had me in some kind of trance.

"Plato," he said before he released his grip. "What are you doing out here?"

"Nobody calls me that anymore," I said.

"I haven't seen you in forever, brother." He always called people "brother" for some reason. It made me suspicious. "The last time I saw you, we were on Eastern Standard Time. You lived in that place above the laundromat. By the lake."

"Yeah," I confirmed, thinking about that apartment in Sherwood, New York.

"Do you still talk to Chaz and Lou?"

"Not for a long time."

"How long ago was that? Like, five years?"

"Eight."

"Eight goddamn years?" He leaned back as if the information might tip him over. "Jesus Christ."

"Have a seat," I told him.

He sat down across from me with his back to an empty frame that used to hold a mirror. Someone had removed the glass, leaving nothing but an ornate rectangle hanging on the wall. Because the glass was missing, I could only guess whether Jack's hair was starting to thin on top. I handed him the cigarette I had just rolled.

"Can we smoke in here?" he asked, looking toward the NO SMOKING sign near the entrance.

"You aren't supposed to," I told him, "but they let me."

I lit his cigarette, and the waitress approached our table.

"You can't smoke in here," she said.

Jack said something to her in the same language she and the cook used to speak to each other.

"I guess it's fine," she replied with a shrug and walked away.

I rolled myself another cigarette and lit it. I was near the end of the pouch of Bugler, so the tobacco was stale. Yellow flecks stuck to my lips and the side of my mouth and left a bitter taste on my tongue. I spit them onto the table while Jack hacked his way through the cigarette.

"I haven't smoked one of these in years," Jack said.

We coughed and tried to blow smoke rings, and I asked what he was he was doing in Illinois. He claimed to be working for a small PR firm. He said the job was supposed to be temporary, and that once he landed a gig managing a hedge fund, he and his girlfriend were going to get married.

"She used to be a model," he said. "But now she's getting into acting."

"You're a couple of thousand miles short of LA," I said.

"There's a lot going on in Chicago," he explained. "A lot."

We were a long way from Chicago too, but I didn't say anything. I told him a little bit about my research. He seemed interested in it—almost too interested. I managed to keep the discussion vague enough that he wouldn't know how much I knew or how close I was to the Unified Theory.

"Can you believe we ran into each other?" he asked after I'd explained the connections between gold-backed currency systems and the assassination of public figures. "I mean, of all people, I never thought I'd see you again."

"My life is full of mysteries and coincidences," I told him, which was true. Then I said, "Nothing surprises me anymore," which was also true.

"You are a total fucking trip, man," he said and wiped his lips to remove the tobacco that was stuck to them. "Remember all those parties we used to go to back when you lived by the lake?"

"Did we go to parties together?" I asked.

He didn't respond. It was like he hadn't heard me. He just started telling stories about the old days: "Oh, God. Remember how Chaz always got that insane weed?"

"It was pretty good weed," I admitted.

"And that girl who was always around," he said. "The mousy one."

"Melanie?"

"No. That wasn't it. The one with the stupid, round face."

"Kim?" I asked, not sure who else it could be.

"The one with the short hair. The boy cut."

"The only one I remember with a boy cut was Esther."

"Esther!" he said and smacked his hands together. "That's it."

"You couldn't remember Esther's name?"

"I haven't seen her in years."

"You two were dating."

"That didn't keep you from trying to hit on her."

I didn't know what to say to that. I had thought this detail might not be mentioned, but here we were discussing it. I knew he was lying about not remembering her name. I smoked my cigarette and tried to think of why he might lie about that.

"Did you ever hook up with her?" Jack asked, his face expectant. He was angling for something. He was going to ask me about what happened at the lake the night before we tried to get into Club 137. He was going to ask me about the UFO I saw. It must have been the only thing he could think about from the moment he'd found me.

"I haven't seen her in a long time," I said.

"Right, right," he said, playing it cool. "Hey, do you still have back problems?" he asked.

"Sometimes," I said, "but lately it's been great. I've been taking these homeopathic remedies, sucking on colloidal silver. It works pretty awesome."

The waitress and the short-order cook continued to watch us as we smoked one cigarette after another, and Jack talked on and on about that weird summer we'd spent in Sherwood. It actually would've been nice to reminisce about those times if I had been with anyone but Jack.

I have trouble remembering my past. Sometimes I remember something having happened to me, but my sister says it actually happened to my brother. Sometimes I wonder if she is working with them to try to abscond with my memories. Like the time I lost my shoes rolling down a hill or the time my dad and I rescued a goose from the median of the highway. Ever since the accident it's been like that, like everyone wants to move my memories around. But I remember everything about that summer in Sherwood when Lou and Chaz and I saw those flashing lights in the sky.

Sherwood was in upstate New York, the armpit of the Adirondack Mountains, beside some train tracks that led to a hollowed-out turbine plant. We all loved the place and wanted desperately to leave it.

We'd all grown up in town, but I was older than Lou and Chaz by a couple of years. They were in the same graduating class and talked about high school as if they had been in Iraq together.

I was stuck in Sherwood because my band, Suicidal Child, had taken off for California without me. The guitar player had thought he could sing, and I guess he'd decided to find out. It's not like I still hold a grudge or anything. I mean, I get it. But I don't have to like it.

So I was still in town with the rest of the burnouts. The three of us moved in together, into that place above the laundromat. Lou and I were the first ones in, and then Chaz agreed to take the third bedroom. The place was falling apart and smelled, but it was also walking distance from the lake where we went swimming.

I liked Lou because he was a film buff and knew all this trivia about how a movie was different from the book and who was originally supposed to be in a certain role before "creative differences" necessitated a change. Lou talked a lot about going to film school, but he got sad anytime you asked him about it. "I need to make my films outside any kind of system," he would say.

Chaz was a schemer, always trying to worm his way into something or other, but he was a good guy when he had to be.

We swam in the lake all summer, so we didn't have to shower. None of us brushed our teeth or combed our hair either. We wore sunscreen instead of deodorant—until I found out how much oxybenzone the government put into it. We stole cable from the neighbors, and I was just starting to recognize which pop stars were using ritual magic to hypnotize us all and which ones were trying to break away and tell the world the truth.

Sometimes Lou and I would wander around the campus of the nearby college, the one none of us could afford to attend. All the buildings were adorned with ancient occult symbols, and I would tell the clueless students what the letters and characters carved into the cement really meant and how the place had been built on secret societies and black magic. When it was too hot to do anything else, we would spend the day in the air-conditioned university library, hunting through the stacks. I would steal books that had been donated by esoteric groups to see if I could find clues to their master plans encoded somewhere deep in the texts. Lou would use his fingernails to peel the electronic tags from the books to help me smuggle them from the library, and I would add them to my collection back at the apartment.

At night Lou, Chaz, and I used to sneak onto the public beaches at the lake, dodging the cops on their ATVs, slipping into the water undetected. We'd climb the lifeguard chairs and get high and stare out over the water. Some nights the moon and the stars would be so bright that we could read the books of poetry we always carried with us. We would read them aloud and memorize verses so we could try them out on girls. Other nights the sky was so black none of us could see anything. Those nights we would tell each other every secret we could think of, speaking them into the darkness.

Lou loved the water the most.

"Come on, Plato," he'd say to me. "Let's go down to the lake."

I'd agree, and we'd try to get Chaz to come along. It was hard to convince him to go. He always wanted to stay and mess around with Kim, the hot chick from upstairs. She would come down to our apartment all the time. We had this poster on the wall, the kind that looks like a random pattern until you unfocus your gaze and an image appears. We would tell Kim you could see an airplane if you looked hard enough, and she would say, "Oh yeah. I see it," and we would laugh because really it was a shark. Then we would watch a Stanley Kubrick movie, and Lou would tell us how the movie was different from the book. Sometimes, when the lights were out, Kim would give Chaz a hand job right there in the living room with everyone. The rest of us acted like we didn't know it was happening. It was awkward, but I didn't care.

I didn't care about much that summer. Even the break-in didn't bother me. We came home from the lake one day to find the place an even bigger wreck than usual. There wasn't much to steal, but they did get their hands on some documents I was hiding under my mattress. I'm pretty sure the documents were the reason for the break-in. My copies of *Covert Action* were gone, along with my books on the new evolution and my CDs on freeing yourself from media mind control. The fact that they were stolen proved I was on to something. Up until the B&E, which the cops did fuck-all about, I'd been lying to myself about man's essential goodness and the benefits of Marxist communal living, but after those buzzards broke in, I couldn't believe in that stuff anymore.

I didn't mourn the loss of my childish innocence for too long, though. As a matter of fact, a week after the break-in, we threw a pretty kick-ass party. We couldn't afford a keg, but we got a case of beer and some liquor. Lou played bartender, and I made up names for all the drinks, like an Illuminat-ini, which was a mudslide but with gin instead of Kahlúa, and Chaz tried to teach everyone dance moves they already knew. It was a good time, but most importantly—from my perspective at least—Esther showed up.

I was in the kitchen, sipping a watered-down drink Lou had made, when I heard Kim explaining the poster to Esther.

"It's an airplane," Kim said.

"I don't see it," Esther told her.

I was watching from across the apartment, trying to think of something to say to Esther. She didn't talk a lot, but I could tell by her eyebrows that she had an opinion about everything. People always talk about the eyes being the "windows to the soul," but really it's the eyebrows. Hers twisted into crazy formations whenever anyone said something dumb. I felt like we were both suspicious of things others took for granted and that maybe we should talk about that.

She would never admit it, but Esther had been a goth in high school; complete with black makeup, torn fishnet stockings, and Siouxsie and the Banshees t-shirts. She'd grown out of it, of course, but she never lost the somber, sad-eyed look that went with all the vampiric posturing.

It was that look—resigned to disappointment but still fed up with all the bullshit—that captivated me. It was like she knew the world could do better but had gotten used to seeing it fail. She also still wore these round eyeglasses that I knew were fake.

I made my way over to the poster, making it impossible for Kim not to introduce me.

"Do you know Plato?" she asked Esther.

"We went to school together, right?" Esther said to me.

It was like being asked if I drank purified water and ate non-GMO food.

Kim floated away, as she was wont to do. I tried to be cool about being alone with Esther, but I wasn't. I even tried out some of the poetry I had memorized. She didn't seem impressed, but she didn't seem to mind either. I'd seen her around a lot with Jack, but maybe she was sick of that smug smile and perfect hair, those high-school-quarterback shoulders. Maybe she was looking for something else.

We talked for a while. Esther seemed sad even though she was smiling.

"You know any place to go besides here?" she asked.

We snuck away without telling anyone. It was a dark night: no stars, no moon. When we got to the lake, we looked down at the water's flat surface, but we couldn't see our reflections. We took off our clothes and swam together, and everything changed. She smiled a little bigger. I could smell the pheromones the trees were sending to one another. I could sense what Esther was feeling because the water connected us. My back even stopped hurting.

When we swam to shore, I let Esther get ahead of me

so I could watch her climb out of the water. Her body looked as dark and smooth as the lake, and the blond highlights in her hair were like the tips of waves. She acted like she didn't know I was watching her even as she let me watch her.

"Why do they call you Plato?" she asked when I sat down next to her on the wet sand.

"Don't ask me," I replied. "That's Lou's thing."

She laughed. I knew she was forming an opinion about me, but I trusted her. That's what that night was doing for us.

"So, what's up with you and Jack?" I asked, feeling like we had reached a point where I could ask her that.

"Let's not talk about Jack," she said.

We lay on the beach and stared up at the starless sky. She had taken off those fake glasses and put them next to her clothes, and she didn't pretend to squint or struggle to see. That, too, made me trust her. I'm pretty sure she left those glasses there on the beach that night.

"I know why you didn't go to LA," she said.

Everyone knew how the other members of Suicidal Child had left without me. "Who wants to go to LA anyway?" I said. "That place is gonna slide into the ocean."

"No," she said. "I mean, I know about the accident."

"Yeah," I told her. "It really put me in a predicament. But my back is feeling a lot better lately. I am doing these yogic breathing exercises that are really great."

We stopped talking, and I thought about kissing her, but I couldn't remember how to lift my body into a position to do it, what muscles I would even use. I continued to think about this until I could tell it had been too long since I'd spoken, and it would be weird to kiss her after such a long silence. We stayed until the night got too cold. (For a while I hoped irrationally that it would warm up again.) Then we returned to the party, which was still happening but with new people, new ideas, new problems.

Lou and Chaz looked at me different now, as if something had shifted. They were both kind of pissed that I'd taken Esther to the lake at night, because that was our secret thing. They tried to give me a hard time when I told them nothing had happened between me and her, but I didn't listen to them. Just because nothing happens when you are out swimming with a girl, it doesn't always mean she doesn't like you. Sometimes it means she does.

I told Lou and Chaz they were being bitches, and they acted like they had let it go, but I knew they thought I had betrayed some unspoken pact.

The night we saw the UFO, Chaz had been trying to get us to go to a bar. It was near the end of the summer, and we were worn out from sun and parties, so Lou and I didn't want to go, but Chaz was insistent. Lou told him he would go if we stopped by the lake first for a quick swim. We could still get to the bar by 10 PM, he said. "Plato will come, too," Lou promised, as if throwing me in to sweeten the deal.

"I'm doing research," I said, fast-forwarding through several music videos I had taped off of television.

"Come on," Lou said. "The weather's only nice for like six weeks every summer."

I followed along with them while Chaz complained about everything: the temperature, Lou's smelly jacket, the break-in, the fact that I had brought Esther to the beach. He even got pissed at me for how I was walking: "Would you stop limping? It's your back that you pretend hurts, not your leg, remember?"

"I'm not pretending."

We walked down the sidewalk against the crowds of people heading for the burger place, the bars, and Club 137, the one dance club in all of Sherwood. All the people on the street seemed stupid to me, so busy obeying the rules. Their lives were meaningless.

When we got to the lake, I was glad I had come. We took off our clothes and jumped in the water. I can't remember if we were high or not, but I remember the lake wrapping around my body like a cool hand. I knew we had made the right decision.

That was when I saw it. We all did—the glowing lights hovering above the water, casting no reflection on its surface. They moved in unison, like a constellation that had been torn from the heavens and was being dragged across the lake. No one spoke. Then the lights were gone. They just disappeared.

None of us remembered swimming back to shore. We just found ourselves standing on the sand, dry and fully dressed. We left the beach and discovered the town was empty, as if everyone had given up on getting drunk or laid and gone home. There were no cars double-parked on the street, no music pouring from the open windows of the apartment buildings, no packs of well-muscled boys, no musicians with guitar cases flopped open. The bars were all closed. Lou tried to call someone, but his phone was acting weird. Finally, we found a drunk guy talking to Kim. He thought she was a hooker, but I knew she was just trying to pick his pocket.

"What time is it?" we asked.

"Time to take a walk," the drunk guy said to us while he tried to sniff her hair.

Kim said it was 3 AM. We had somehow lost the whole evening to the flashing lights in the sky. We looked at each other as Kim walked away with the drunk guy, her hand tucked inside his back pocket.

The next night we were at a party. Lou had told me that Esther would probably be there, and she was, but Jack was there, too, lurking nearby whenever I tried to talk to her. That was the night we all tried to get into that stupid dance club, the 137. Jack said he knew someone who worked there who could get us in. We stood around outside while Jack went in and out of a service door, trying to find his friend.

I wanted to go to a dive bar where we could eat day-old chicken sandwiches and play foosball.

"I don't see myself in a place like this," I told Esther after Jack left us standing on the sidewalk a third time. "Let's go to Donavan's."

Esther didn't say anything. She just folded her arms to protect herself from the chill and watched Jack talking to the guy he knew. We could hear him tell the guy that we had girls with us, which was true, sort of. There was Esther, and this girl who was a little overweight, and Lou had his arm around a girl whose teeth were messed up. It would have been nice to have Kim with us. They probably would have let us right in if she had been there. But she and Chaz were somewhere else—probably hooking up back at our place.

"We won't have to wait out on the sidewalk at

Donavan's," I told Esther. "We can go right in."

"What about Jack?" she asked.

"Every time he goes in there, it takes him longer to come back. I think that guy is giving him shots while we stand here in the cold."

"We can't just leave him," Esther said.

That was so like her. She had a big heart.

Jack came back and told us the guy was working on getting our names on the list. I could smell the booze on his breath. He turned and started talking with this loud guy in line behind us, as if he knew him.

"I told you he was getting drunk," I said to Esther.

"We're all drunk," she said.

I leaned close to Esther and whispered that she should come with me to the lake.

Jack turned around. "Are you hitting on my girl, brother?" he said, and he laughed like nothing had any value, like everything was a joke. It made me want to punch him or kick him in the side of the knee. (I never did learn to fight.)

"Meet me at the water," I told Esther, not whispering anymore.

"Where you saw the UFO?" Jack said.

"How do you know about that?" I asked.

"Because you haven't shut up about it all summer."

"It only just happened yesterday."

"You can call me tomorrow," Esther said to me, hoping to end the argument.

"I can't. My phone hasn't worked since we saw those lights. You have to meet me where we went swimming. Do you know where I'm talking about?"

"Yeah," she said.

"Be there in thirty minutes," I said, and I turned to leave, feeling like she and I had already tugged each other's clothes off; like we were already post-coital and laughing about some shared joke, maybe the look on Jack's face when I'd told her to meet me at the beach. That's how sure I was that she was going to be there.

Then the guy Jack had been talking to in line stepped out in front of me, blocking my path like he wanted to speak to me. I don't remember being drunk or high, but that is the only explanation I can come up with for why I didn't see Jack circling around to my blind side to punch me in the spine. It felt like he used an energy weapon on me. I don't know where he would have gotten one at that time, but he must have known someone who knew someone, because the pain wasn't localized to my back. I could feel the electric current in my teeth. My tongue tasted like it had been crop-dusted with metallic fibers. I hit the pavement and heard everyone in line laughing. I was sure Esther wasn't, but I didn't want her to see me like this, so I rolled into the alley to catch my breath and assess whether paralysis might set in.

The next thing I remember is stumbling through the streets toward the beach where Chaz and Lou and I had seen the flashing lights. When I got there, the cops were waiting for me. It was like the buzzards knew I was coming. I tried to sneak away and warn Esther that it wasn't safe, but they got me. They told me I was "acting erratically," which I definitely wasn't, and that I was not responding to their commands, which I totally was. Then they smashed my face into the sand.

"Been drinking tonight, sir?" one cop asked. He said "sir" like he knew I would rather he have called me a "dirtbag" so I could feel morally superior. I wanted to come up with some awesome response like: "Just doing a little bird watching," but I only told him my back hurt as he clicked the handcuffs around my wrists.

They made me wait in the car forever, and then they took me to the station and processed me. Eventually, they charged me with trespassing and some other nonsense.

I wondered who had told them about the UFO and what the cops had hoped to find at the beach. I'm sure they turned up nothing. Space aliens know better than to get caught by stupid local cops.

"Remember that time we went to the beach and saw that UFO?" Jack asked, looking over the menu in the diner.

Every once in a while I would look up at the empty frame where there used to be a mirror and expect to see my reflection in it, but then I would remember there was nothing there. I wished they'd just take the damn thing down.

The waitress stood near the coffee machine and watched us. I wasn't sure where the cook had gone, but I was sure he was watching us, too.

"UFO?" I said to Jack.

"You gotta remember the UFO. It was crazy."

"Yeah," I said, "but you weren't there."

"What are you talking about? We saw it together. My phone never worked right after that."

I wondered what his angle was. Had Lou or Chaz sent him to find me? Was he freelancing for the Feds? Working for someone far more nefarious? Had they showed him the file they had on me? Did he really believe he had been there that night?

"Yeah," I told him, finishing my coffee and snuffing out a cigarette that I hadn't rolled too well to begin with. "That UFO was crazy."

I thought about Esther. The last time I'd seen her was standing outside of that club.

"I did hook up with Esther Shelton," I told Jack. "We hooked up the night you were trying to get everyone into Club 137."

"Oh, shit," he said. "That club was crazy."

"Yeah."

"Great mojitos."

"I guess."

"You know, it's good to see you doing so well. I know things were hard for you after the car accident. All that medical stuff, not to mention the legal stuff."

"Then don't mention it."

"Hey, brother, I know it was an accident, even if the guy's family couldn't see it that way."

It was then I decided that he had been in on it. He had too much info not to have been in on it. He may have even set me up to cause that accident. He was certainly the one who had kept me and Esther apart. I wondered what he'd done with her. I wondered if he was the one who'd broken into our place. He must have contacted the Feds and had the police cordon off the lake that night. They had probably sent him, all these years later, to figure out what I knew and maybe to tie up loose ends. Why else was he so far from Sherwood?

When the waitress came to check on us, Jack spoke to her in a language that was definitely not English and might not have been Spanish either. It may have been Latin. I let him buy me lunch because I figured if I was being tracked, I might as well get a sandwich out of the deal. We talked and smoked cigarettes for another half-hour while I tried to get as much information from him as I could. I figured he was so dumb that he might reveal the whole plan to me, but apparently his handlers knew how unreliable he was and had wisely kept him on a need-to-know basis. He tried again to ask me about the accident, but I just fed him some lies of my own; it was hard to tell if he fell for any of them. He told me this unbelievable cover story about these meetings he had started going to that had helped him come to a lot of realizations, and how he was sorry for some of the things he had done and said to me back then. He asked for my number and said he was going to call me.

We shook hands, and I left. As soon as I was out of sight of the Nite Owl, I started to run. While I ran, I tore up all of my research from that day. I left it in shreds in the street. If I'd had the time, I would have burned it. I knew my sister's apartment would be the first place they would look for me, so I turned down an avenue I had never seen before. I hustled through the streets until my lungs hurt and my legs threatened to give out. I wasn't sure where I was, but I didn't care. I could see the Patterns in the way the houses had been built and in the shapes of the bushes; in the names of the streets and the position of the moon. It was all there, just waiting for me to figure it out.

THE BEDWETTERS

Part III: Once School Started Again / Exploring Warbly Forest

Dad always watched the six o'clock news even though he hated it. He would stand there in front of the television, holding the remote like a pistol ready to be fired while I set the table and Mom peeled the tops off the Tupperwares. While Mom and I bowed our heads and prayed, Dad would argue with the local cops, so-called experts, and corrupt politicians talking on the television screen. He offered wry comments like, "Yeah, right!" and "I bet you would" anytime one of them spoke.

Because no one knew what to talk about once he finally sat down, I could tell she was going to the doctor again. The salad bowl was passed without comment, and I could tell by the twist of my father's face that he was trying to lodge a silent complaint about the way my mother chewed. He sighed and scoffed and wiped his mouth. She rolled her eyes and twisted her fingers into strange, little configurations in her lap.

I hoped they wouldn't talk to me, but my mother smiled and asked me if I had finished my homework. She asked in a way that seemed designed to instruct my father on how civilized people communicated.

"I didn't have any homework, so I spent some time in Warbly Forest," I told her.

Warbly Forest wasn't really a forest, but that's what everyone called the little patch of trees between Wednesday Avenue and the old post office where the kids in my neighborhood used to play.

"You know I don't like you back there all by yourself," Mom said. "Kids get kidnapped."

Dad didn't say anything. His eyes were already sinking. He was already using the silverware very carefully, like he was just learning to operate the utensils, knocking over glasses and clattering the knife onto the plate as if it weighed hundreds of pounds. Even though the sun wasn't even down yet, he was already doing that thing where my mother would talk to him, and he wouldn't answer until she said his name six or seven times.

"School is just school," I told Mom, trying to pull her attention away from him, trying to tell her the truth without telling her anything. "And Mr. Morales is fine now. He isn't giving me any problems anymore. Not really."

My mother looked at me but turned her head so that her ear pointed at my father, who had groaned into the kitchen. He had given up on us in favor of looking into the refrigerator, staring into the appliance like there were entire worlds inside the squeaking, cream-colored box. We all listened to the hum of the thing for what seemed like a long time. Little puffs of cold air reached from the machine, grasping for my father but dissolving before they touched him. I wondered if he was really looking for anything or if maybe he just liked the feel of the cool air on his hot face.

"Mr. Morales said that I should try doing breathing exercises," I lied. "He said it might help with the bedwetting. Because wetting the bed in third grade is one thing, but fourth grade?"

"I'm glad he knows how special you are," she said and smiled, but I wasn't so sure.

After dinner my mother went to her doctor's appointment, and my father passed out, still in his boots, while the nine o'clock news soldiered on without him. He hated the news even more the second time around, but at least he knew what to expect by that point. Hours later I heard my mother return home and click her tongue upon finding him unconscious in his chair. She groaned while she tugged on his limbs, hoping to lever him to his feet, or at least wake him enough to stumble him up the steps and into their bed. His weight was such that when he stood, he made the entire house moan. When he walked, each step he took crashed with a force that shook the pictures on the wall and knocked alarm clocks and desk lamps from their assigned locations on dressers and end tables.

I fell asleep to the sounds of him collapsing into bed, and I dreamed of flying high above the earth while a shadow-colored shape on the ground tugged at me like I was a kite. The shadow was jealous of my height and wanted my position, and it scraped at me from far below. I wet right through the comforter that night.

Parts V-VII: Exploring the House

I could hear them in the basement, arguing. I pressed my ear against the floor and listened, trying to hear if my name was vibrating up through the frame of the house, if it was me they were shouting about. I couldn't pick out any words, though, just the low bark of my father and the cold, murmuring resentment of my mother.

When my mother left, I heard the soft, sad sound of the wheels of her car coasting slowly into the street, the headlights making a wild UFO arc across the ceiling and walls. Dad came up to my room. I closed my eyes and pretended to sleep, but I could hear him breathing from the doorway to my bedroom, and I could smell him, the dull stink of vodka working its way past the smell of diesel fuel and spearmint gum.

I kept my eyes closed and waited for him to leave. I didn't move until I heard him in the bathroom, hocking a loogie into the bowl as he pissed, the stream long and proud, crackling against the porcelain like static from the radio. He sang an old R&B song while he peed, and the strength of his micturition didn't wane until he got to the chorus.

Once he returned to his chair and passed out, I crept downstairs. I edged along the wall like it was the border between Warbly Forest and the Spadaros' backyard. I could see him asleep and spilling from his chair, his limbs wild like the La-Z-Boy had erupted him. With Mom gone and Dad snoring in the television room, I had the same feeling I did when I found the amazing treasures buried in the dirt in Warbly Forest.

Treasures like:

- Bullet casings gathered near the north end. (The shells were not from a mobilized militia intent upon taking over the town by force, but instead left over from a group of high schoolers who would split a six-pack and act like they were drunk when they shot off an almost harmless .22.)

- A piece of plywood nailed to a tree. I imagined that it hid the entrance to a hideout of a criminal enterprise, a band of gangsters who would torture me if they found out how much I knew. (In reality it was just the never-finished tree house project of Jonathan Hunzicker and his father, which they had abandoned long before Jonathan went away to college.)
- Brad Culver's cousin making out with Sean Bellanger.
- Denis Laughlin's dad in his loosened tie, talking to himself, actually pacing, pulling at his hair, some problem of the adult world eating him from the inside.

The pornographic magazines were easily the most significant discovery, however. I found them obscured by a heap of half-dead plants. The magazines had been stolen, used, and then destroyed, as was the custom. The pile, probably once belonging to one of my neighbors' dads, bloomed with colors, and the pages wilted around the edges. I plucked one like it was some renegade fruit and sprinted it back home, cradling the purloined dirty magazine as I would a wounded pet, a puppy whose paw was bit by a snake. I realized once I was safe in my room that the porno I had uncovered from the earth was pulsing with the slick squirm of a wave of tiny beetles. I dusted them from my arms, terrified for a moment, then fascinated. I retrieved a can of bug spray from the kitchen to kill all the vermin. The naked bodies of the men and the tones of the women seemed to glisten from the poison being applied, the incident resulting in me associating the scent of Raid ever after with ejaculation.

While I was scraping those bugs off that magazine, I felt like something was opening up before me. Like I had something to myself. Something to examine. Something I should leave alone but knew I couldn't.

So that's how I felt when I looked at our house that night when Mom left, and Dad was passed out on the couch, and I was left alone to explore. I could see it anew. I saw it the way a stranger might—all its messes, its flaws, what it lacked, and how it smelled. I saw all the zones where random objects accumulated, corners and angles that we had all silently agreed we would avoid. I saw the lack of comfortable furniture or bright colors, the chaos coming from the dirty Tupperware in the sink, and I smelled the acrid scent of expired meat decomposing in the garbage among the coffee grounds and dripping beer cans.

I saw all the colors, how they really were.

The dining room was wide open and lush, the furniture towering, the little drawers in the hutch where Mom kept the plates and cloth napkins plump with possibility, bursting and comely. I slid the china around, looking for some hidden treasure that hadn't been there when I'd been tasked with setting the table last Thanksgiving.

My father still snored away, and so I went into the refrigerator. I stared into it the way he usually did, looking for desserts. The closest thing I could find was one of Mom's strictly off-limits, low-calorie yogurts. In the pantry I found a tube of frosting. I uncapped it and squirted the thick goo into my mouth. It didn't taste like anything, but the texture felt good on my tongue. I found in the junk drawer almost nothing that wasn't broken or corroded. Something had leaked and covered the bottom of the drawer in a brown, jagged stain. I pulled a flashlight from the drawer, but it was out of batteries. I couldn't remember a time when it had had batteries, but I checked anyway.

I entered the basement, my father's territory, carrying that non-operational flashlight like it was a sword. The basement was a strange chaos of metal, glass, and chipped paint that I didn't dare touch for fear that some symbiotic link between them and my father would alert him to my intrusion. Curled hunks of sawdust like shed snakeskin accumulated on the ground, and I tried not to nudge a single spiral. The argument he had had with Mom was draped over everything.

I looked around and breathed in the cold, cement stink, the strange must, and bitter, metallic taste of the tools that hung in the air. I thought I heard crying working its way through the walls. I could see the circuit box from across the room, the command center where Dad would go to reset things when we blew a fuse—sometimes he'd solve the problem possessed by a fit of excitement, other times he would descend to his station molten with anger.

I climbed onto the workbench and balanced myself on the toolbox where he hid his vodka so I could peer into the metal circuit box. It ended up being merely a series of what looked like large light switches. Each switch had a different label like "FRONT" and "2nd" and "Foyer." I wasn't sure what a foyer was, but I was pretty sure we didn't have one. I flipped the switch for the basement and turned out all the lights around me. I was filled, briefly, with the familiar burst of nausea I associated with the power to control the electricity to the entire house. I began flipping the switches, every one except the switch labeled

BASEMENT, the authority making me irrational, but I soon stopped and flipped them back the way they were. Without being able to see the effect of my actions, the authority felt useless. I sulked my way back to the first floor; the only remnant of my handiwork was that all the digital clocks flashed "12:00" over and over as if it were the only thing they could remember.

I climbed the stairs to the second floor and stopped to look out the window at Warbly Forest. I wondered what manner of strange undulations were happening on the forest floor and in the bark of the trees without me.

My parents' bedroom was the biggest room upstairs, but it was just as cramped as all the rooms in the house, all the furniture and possessions cinched together like pendants crowded on a string. The wallpaper was drooping in places, and sometimes late at night I could hear a calloused hand scrape across the wall to put a wayward strip back into place. There were pictures on the wall, the same ones that had been there since we moved in. There was one of my father, mustachioed and thin, with his arm around my mother.

"I hate that one because my eyes are half closed in it," my mother reported anytime she caught me looking at the photograph. Though she didn't like it, I did. They looked happy in it.

Their bed was a four-poster that my grandfather had made. My father was strangely nostalgic about such things, and so he would not get rid of it even though it creaked every time anyone got into it, rolled out of it, or made any sort of maneuver in it; their infrequent lovemaking was publicized throughout the house with every occurrence. I was strictly banned from the bed and had been for some time, so I knew not to touch the perfectly tucked duvet for fear of leaving evidence that I had been snooping in their room.

I looked under the bed, where there were carefully marked boxes of past years' taxes, and I looked under the dresser. The dresser's wood was gold and soggy. It looked like a pastry, the drawers overstuffed with ill-fitting shirts and outdated fashions. I opened the underwear drawers, where I found my father's stained boxer shorts, my mother's lacy underwear, and a box of condoms from when my mother had to go off the birth control for reasons I didn't understand but had heard them discussing. I was disappointed to find nothing new but a few balled-up socks. I don't know what I had hoped to find—maps to hidden treasure, bags and bags of candy the likes of which we only had on Halloween, action figures or baseball cards that they had forgotten to give me for Christmas, or even flashlight batteries.

When I opened the closet I found what I expected, which were my mother's floor-length dresses, my father's collection of ties that he never wore anymore but that I continued to add to—because what else was I supposed to give him for Christmas?—and a too-large pile of shoes that seemed extravagant for people who referred to themselves as lower-middle-class Democrats.

Beyond their respective wardrobes, in between my father's cowboy boots from when he was in a band and my mother's red high heels that I was sure she had worn, but never when I was looking, was the small box full of all manner of riches, most of which I could not comprehend.

You won't believe me, but there was all kinds of stuff

back there:

A box full of books, the titles of which I did not understand. I would heft each one and read and reread the title, hoping this time it might eventually reveal itself to me. I would open the book to an early page and try to read it, but the long, Latin-built words were parapets set up to surround the information stored within. I would open another book, one full of medical procedures, one with pictures of animal attacks, and another about attaching prosthetics. The people in the photos gazed out from the books, their eyes drooping and weary. They all looked familiar though I had never met any of them.

A bag that was filled with different kinds of money. U.S. currency, the grotesque and stoic faces of history staring out from them; Canadian currency, which I recognized from when Heather Longo came back from her grandmother's and wouldn't shut up about all the loonies and toonies she had; and currencies that I couldn't possibly identify and were oddly shaped and full of as many colors as the dirty magazines I had found in Warbly forest. I lifted the thick, rubber-banded packs of money from the bag and sniffed them like people did in the movies, but they didn't smell like anything.

A knife. The handle lurid and black and each serrated notch seeming to want to bite my flesh. It looked like the one wielded by the hero of an R-rated movie I had secretly watched and even more secretly been terrified of. The knife felt as heavy as I assumed a gun would be. It made me wonder if a gun might be so heavy that I would not be able to lift it. I looked around the closet for a gun but could not find one. All I found was a box of Mom's medical records. I didn't want to read them, but I did.

I don't know why I saw the door that time and never before. Maybe it was something about the way I stood or the way the closet was arranged that allowed me to see it. Or maybe I had just never known to look at the back wall of the closet where there was a doorknob staring out like an indifferent, cycloptic eyeball.

The door seemed like the kind of secret that needed to remain hidden. I placed my ear against it like it was the chest of a lover, and I listened, but the only sound I heard was the sound of Mom's car pulling into the driveway.

I was asleep before she came upstairs, dreaming full-color dreams that I could not understand or interpret. She must have dragged my father up the steps and into their bedroom while I was pissing myself in my slumber. They were both downstairs when I woke up, shuffling around the kitchen, inefficient and clumsy, waiting for their breakfasts and coffees to smooth out their movements.

"The clocks are still all wrong?" Dad asked, though he knew the answer.

Mom dropped me off at school like she always did. She even sang along to the songs on the oldies station and chatted with me about Mr. Morales as if something horrifying and new had not happened to me the night before. We walked around in our own lives like everything was fine. I had to wait a full week until Mom's next doctor's appointment before I was finally able to open the door and investigate what was on the other side.

Part IX: What Mom Knows

At school I asked the other children I knew if they had secret doors and hidden rooms in their houses as well. Brittany Kohler told me that her pet rat had escaped its terrarium, and she could sometimes hear it in the walls. Josh Fugett told me that his older brother lived in his basement, and he could smell him smoking weed and hear him getting drunk down there sometimes. Ani Nagel told me a story that I knew to be the plot of a scary movie.

My parents had stopped talking to one another altogether. Sometimes Dad didn't even sit down for dinner with us. Mom would just sit in her chair and stare out of the window in the dining room while she slowly chewed the crust of the microwave pizza we ate almost every night.

"Do you ever wish I had a brother?" I asked her.

"Maybe before," she said, surprising me with a response. "But not now."

"What would his name be?"

"I'd probably name him after my father," she said. "That's probably what I should have done with you."

The sound of the evening news, and then The History Channel during the commercials, and then the evening news again, washed in from the next room like the waves of a flood. Neither my mother nor I acknowledged it.

"Can I go play in my room?" I asked my mother.

She looked surprised to be interrupted from her thoughts. She uncrossed her legs and then re-crossed them the opposite way.

"What was that?"

"I just want to go play in my room," I said.

"You hardly ate anything," she said.

"I'll eat it upstairs."

"You can't eat in your room," she said as she turned to look out the front window again. "You'll get bugs."

"I've got a can of Raid up there," I explained.

She didn't ask why, and she didn't object when I carried the paper plate full of pizza and soggy breadsticks upstairs.

Part XXX: Getting Picked Up From School

One day near the end of the school year Mr. Morales sent me down to the office. He patted me on the head in a way that annoyed me. It tipped the balance of the whole adversary thing we had going. By the sad way he told me my aunt was picking me up, I could tell there was something wrong. When I made it to the office, I could hear the school nurse talking to someone who was using the Long Island nasal my Dad's sisters used. I tried to peek into the office to see which one it was. Had my aunt Patricia showed up, it probably would have been because of car problems or something like that. But it wasn't my aunt Patricia. It was my aunt Nancy in the office, whispering with the principal and the school nurse, their secrets hissing like tea kettles. If Dad had asked my aunt Nancy to pick me up, it meant something was really wrong.

In the car, my aunt Nancy told me I could put on any radio station I wanted. I flipped the buttons and stopped on a song I knew the kids in my class liked. I didn't like it, but I knew it was something my parents wouldn't have let me listen to in their cars, so I wanted to take the opportunity to do so while I could.

When we got to our house no one was home. My aunt Nancy told me to go play outside. I traversed Warbly Forest the short way and emerged on Wednesday Avenue, but nothing was happening; the street was still and menacing, so I returned to the house and hid near the window to the kitchen and tried to eavesdrop. I could tell she was on the phone with someone, but I could barely hear what she was saying. She was talking quickly and using words I didn't know even though I regularly got red stars for vocabulary and sometimes even got orange stars. I finally gave up and wandered back into Warbly Forest and tried to see if there was anything new out there I could find.

The clouds were writhing in slow motion opposite the sun, the mess of it swirling toward the dusk. When I came back inside my aunt was sitting at the table and looking out the front window the same way my mother sometimes did.

"Your dad will be home at his normal time." She said it like I had asked about him. Like she was annoyed that she had to answer. Then she hugged me, pressing me against her in a way that made it hard to breathe. She kissed me on the cheek and left without saying another word.

Part VIII: What It Was Like Down There

To keep the door from creaking, you can't open it slowly, like you might think—patience and control aren't always the answer. You have to open it as fast as you can, like you are pulling the cord of a lawn mower. You can't give the hinges time to moan and protest. When you open the door, you will see the steps leading down. You will be scared to descend them, even if you've already been down there, but you know you have to do it anyway. You will squat in the closet for as long as it takes to psych yourself up enough to go down there, and then you will enter the door and begin to descend the steps.

When you get to the bottom of the stairs you will be

in a small room, no bigger than a child's bedroom. It will have a concrete floor and wooden studs all along the walls. The floor will be absent of stains and rubble and will feel as newly constructed as the steps. Across the cement of the hidden space is a small cage, and inside the cage is a young boy. He is without clothes except for a pair of plain white underwear. He sits in the cage with his blonde head on his knees. His eyes are animals, scavengers scurrying from a garbage can. When you reach the bottom of the stairs he looks up and barks at you. He seems bored with his antagonism, though. Like he is only doing it because he thinks that is what is expected of him. He remains sitting and tilts his head for a moment before placing it back on his knees.

He looks like he could be in Mr. Morales' class, his gaze drifting from the chalkboard at the front of the class to the window.

When you try to say hello to him he doesn't respond or even look up from his cage.

There isn't a camera in the room or anything, or a door to another room or anything else. It's just you and the boy.

The smell of his urine and excrement lingers, but you cannot see where he goes. There is no toilet or even a bucket in his cage, but he must go somewhere because the smell cannot escape the basement, and it is pervasive. It lives down there with him like a cellmate.

"What are you doing in that cage?" you can ask him, but he won't answer. "Where do you BM? Do you just hold it?" you can ask, but he won't say.

He has a bandage on his cheek and vertical bruises on his chest and shoulders. After you look at him for a long time, he might lurch at you and try to stretch his hand all the way toward you through the bars of the cage. He'll bang his torso against the bars. That's how he got those bruises to begin with. You have to step back a little bit so he can't reach you. You'll learn that lesson the hard way.

In the hidden room, you'll tear off little pieces of pizza and slip them through the bars of the boy's cage. He will reach out without taking his eyes off you and grab the pieces from your hands.

Make sure you bring the dirty magazine with you. Spread it open like you are splitting open the torso of a dissected frog and hold the pages against the bars of his cage. Neither of you will speak while you do this. You will hold it until you think he is done looking, and then you will turn to a new page and hold that one up. You will do that for a long time.

He is surrounded by remnants of food, you will notice. Little candy bars and still-green banana peels, empty bowls, and cups. Someone is feeding him. Someone besides you. You'll try to imagine who it might be who crawls through the back of the closet and descends the stairs to feed this boy. You'll try to figure out where they might have gotten him or what they used him for, but you won't be able to fathom an answer. It'll make you wonder what else you don't know.

Part XXXIII: Trying to Escape the Boy

Once my aunt Nancy was gone I sprinted up the steps and climbed through the door in the closet to go and get the boy. I knew it might be my only chance to help him escape. He let me hold onto his hand. He let his fingers go limp, making a little pile in my fist, and he didn't growl or snap, like usual. I led him up the stairs, walking backwards, while he got used to the new of the stairs, of the light, of the carpet of my parents' room. He just looked around at everything, clearly seeing it all for the first time. The colors, the lights, the still, warm comfort of it all. The weird color of the walls, my Star Wars bedcovers, the television playing softly in the other room.

His mouth dangled open. It was like he was asleep, but his legs were moving, and his eyes were open. I worried as I led him through the house that he might pee or BM in the house, but he didn't. He just looked around, his mouth hanging open, his jaw dangling and wobbling from side to side like crystals from a chandelier.

The television was on and loud. I hadn't remembered leaving it on, but the voices scared the boy. Seeing the boy see everything, seeing the house the way he did, picture frames, my room, the television, changed the way I thought about all of these things. After that I could only see them the way the boy must have.

I carried the pornographic magazine I had found in Warbly Forest because I intended to give it to him to take with him into the forest. I knew if I kept it for too much longer, I would get careless with it and someone would find it, and I would get in trouble for having it. Plus, it was something we had shared, and giving it to him felt like the right thing to do.

When we got to the backyard, the sun was starting to go down. The boy stepped down off the back porch, pressing his bare feet into the grass. He laughed as he did so, pleased with the way the earth molded to his feet and the grass tickled his skin. I led him to the back part of the yard which led out to Warbly Forest, and I stuffed the magazine and a small bag of food into his hands.

"Go ahead," I said to him and motioned to Warbly Forest, where I used to love to play and imagine I was a part of something big and strange. "You're free now."

The boy looked at the trees of Warbly Forest and then looked back at me. I wondered if he even knew what a forest was.

"Go ahead," I said, now yelling. "You've got to escape to the forest. That's where you live now."

It had not occurred to me that he would not want to leave.

He crouched down into the stance he had taken when I had first seen him and he had growled and barked like a dog. He dropped what I had given him and clawed at me. I didn't know what else to do, so I pushed the boy, intending to get him started toward his escape, but instead crumpling him into a ball. He huddled and cried. A cable of drool connected his mouth to the ground, and I stepped back. The boy did not move, and I stepped again and finally fled back into the house.

I climbed the stairs to the second floor, and I looked out the window that overlooked the backyard. I could see him still staring back at the house only feet from Warbly Forest, where I imagined his freedom to be. I knew that he could not see me, but it felt like he could. I wondered if maybe he didn't want his freedom. That possibly he liked living in the basement that made me dizzy just to go down there because of the trapped smell of cut wood and chemicals and the faint smell of urine and bowel movement.

The hours encroached on us until I could hide from 6 PM no more. The sun had begun to look like an ornament on the gloaming, but still the boy huddled in the backyard. I knew that soon Dad would arrive home, he would exit the car, the gravel would complain under his feet as he approached, and he would discover what I had done.

There would be no doubt who had let the boy go. I was the only one home.

I had never done anything so bad. The closest I had ever come to doing something like this was when I lied to my parents about buying firecrackers from the older boys at the end of Wednesday Avenue. Or the time I broke Dad's trophy that he got when he was in high school and was on the best baseball team in the state.

But I knew this was different from those times. I knew this was for real.

When Dad pulled the car into the driveway his headlights would be pointed directly at where the boy was standing. I wondered what Dad would say if he came home and found the boy standing there, shirtless and in his torn underwear, alone in the backyard with porno and food from our pantry in his hand. I realized that I should have given him some clothes to wear. I tried to figure out how much time I had before Dad got home, but no one had fixed the clocks that I had reset when I flipped all the switches in the circuit box. I considered bringing the boy some clothes, but I was afraid that dressing him in the backyard might draw attention. I thought about trying to drag him back into the house and putting him back in his cage, but I was afraid of the way he had swiped at me.

I stood at the window at the top of the stairs and closed my eyes and hoped that maybe when I opened them the boy would be gone. I kept them closed for a long time, and I counted to 100. Usually when someone has you close your eyes and count to 100 you count really fast and maybe skip some numbers because you are so excited to find out what happens when you get to 100, but I didn't do that this time. I counted very slowly and kept my eyes totally shut. Then I counted to 100 again, even slower a second time, then a third. The darkness of having my eyes closed changed to a swirl of colors and then lightness, and I couldn't even remember how dark it was outside or if there were lights on in the house. I opened my eyes and looked out into the backyard, feeling somewhere deep down that the boy would be gone. But when I looked into the backyard the boy was still standing there, chewing on the crackers and fruit snacks I had put into a bag for him. He was looking up at the moon that had replaced the recently downed sun. The boy's head was angled crazy on his neck, as if he was trying to peek beneath the skirt of the sky.

From inside the house, I could hear the television where they were teasing their top stories for the six o'clock news, and I knew my father would be home in time to watch it. I ran down the steps, feeling my stomach lurch as my balance slipped out from under me, but I did not fall. I kept my hand on the wall to steady myself. I didn't know what I would do when I got to the boy. Maybe I could push him back further into the wooded area behind the house. Maybe I could shove him into a dark corner of the yard, near the fence, outside of the beams of my father's headlights. Maybe I could cover him with my body and my father wouldn't think it was him back there, but me.

When I opened the back door and leapt from the porch into the middle of the yard, I thought there would be nothing left of him but the magazine, lying vivid in the dirt, but when I swung the back door open and sprinted out into the yard the boy was still there, staring back at me, his eyes retaining none of the vestiges of what had gone on between us. Dad's headlights swung into the driveway and landed on the backyard, illuminating everything. I don't know what it must have looked like to him.

"What the hell are you doing back there?" he asked, standing behind the swung open car door like he was using it for cover.

We ate Chinese food every night that week, and we tried not to talk to each other. I didn't look up as I chewed on the fried chicken pellets that came with sweet and sour sauce. We never talked about the magazine, Mom, or the boy. After all, what was there to talk about? What could Dad even ask me about any of it? What could he even say?

I remember him looking in on me from the hallway and the way it made me feel. The light made strange, origami-shaped angles against his face. I knew there was something between us now. Something we both knew hung over us but something we could never talk about.

TERMS OF VENERY: ORIGIN, MODALITY, AND DIVERSITY OF METAMORPHOSIS MECHANISMS WITHIN SPECIAL SUB-GROUPS

Abstract:

Event predicated by as yet undetermined factors ascribed in the literature to various potential sources: global temperature increases, the prevalence of various chemical components present in no-longer-used pesticides in the South-East and Mid-West regions, or possibly space aliens. The catalyst for event determined to be urges or needs within special group toward members of venery group sub-category. Phenomenon detected in pods of dolphins, rookeries of albatross, certain shrewdnesses of hominids (primates, apes, and families of humans). Sequelae include transformation, metamorphosis, the formation of a chrysalis, drastic change in size, mobility, diet, sexual proclivity. The permanence of change is undetermined.

Hemimetabolan (progressive changes):

Greg and Jessica had been cycling through the stages of grief for months. Jessica vacillated between acceptance and denial, while Greg continued to return to anger like it was his ancestral home.

"You don't think it's just a superstition?" Jessica asked Greg as he stood in the living room with his back to her so he could gaze out the window at the frantic neighborhood preparing for the apocalypse. "Like 2012?"

"I wouldn't call entomology a superstition," he said, not looking at her.

"I would call this Franz Kafka stuff a little hard to believe," she said.

"No one ever thinks it's going to happen to them."

"Except you. You are sure you will be a dung beetle by noon on Wednesday."

She knew him so well that she could tell he was picturing it happening, envisioning the way his torso might collapse into a thorax, hot wings erupting from his shoulder blades, how he might shrink down to a fraction of his size to become a bug if some enemy so wished it upon him.

"Actually, 11:28 AM," he corrected. "I think they even have it figured down to the second."

She gave up on the television and crossed the living room to join him. She kissed him on the side of his face, denting the soft flesh of his cheek. She looked at him as he stared out of the window. His face was misshapen, lopsided, like it had been composited from slices of other, more handsome faces. She liked the way he looked, though. Like some lonely rock, poking out of the middle of a lake.

"At least we won't have to rent that U-Haul," Greg said. They had already decided to move when the news broke, despite the protests of Jessica's teenaged daughter, Cheyanne. After a perceived slight from his manager, Greg had applied to every job in his time zone and had been shocked to be interviewed and hired for one in the next state over. After a considerable amount of debate, he had decided to take it. Cheyanne had been upset and Jessica had told her it wasn't the end of the world. Then the news said otherwise.

"Do you really think it will happen?" she asked Greg as they stared out onto what was once their neighborhood.

"I don't know," Greg answered, looking at Dr. Utley on the TV. "Would they let a guy like this on TV if it wasn't true?"

Dr. Bernard Utley had become something of a national celebrity in the weeks leading up to the event. The hemipterologist, preeminent in his field all his life, had been the one to reveal the coming catastrophe and he became the person most major news outlets turned to for soundbites to fill up the time of their broadcasts. Even with the End approaching, machines like cable news and ad-revenue-supported-content continued; already paid-for commercials for pantyliners and orange juice played in between dire warnings from theoretical statisticians and government officials.

Utley again and again urged people to resist the impetus to act, even if it seemed that taking advantage of the situation might result in what appeared to be a benefit. He cited the risks to oneself and others if a person were to take the opportunity to make that terrible wish and at that precise second transform someone into a swarm of bugs.

Jessica turned off the television. She joined Greg and both stared out the window at their neighbors, some of whom might, within 48 hours, be irrevocably transformed into winged insects with mouthparts designed for piercing and sucking and some of whom, they'd been assured by Dr. Utley, might take the opportunity to do the transforming. The suburbanites scurried around and made their own preparations for the Metamorphosis. Greg and Jessica could see the recently retired couple tottering around their single-level home, while the guy who washed his truck every Saturday was unloading stuffed garbage bags from his front door. He carried them out, one after the other, like the curb was a wound and only overfull garbage bags could do the clotting. The woman with six kids surveyed the neighborhood from her roof, smoking, while her kids throbbed within.

"I hate bugs," Jessica said, still looking out at the panicked neighborhood.

"I know this about you."

"I even hate butterflies. Their weird wings."

"You'd maybe better get used to them."

"Did I ever tell you about the moths?"

"I think I'd remember that."

"This was right after I got thrown out of my dad's house. I remember sitting in there, the cable wasn't even hooked up yet. I was just sitting in the place with all my boxes, staring at the blank screen and there was a moth on top of it. Just one moth that first day, just sitting on the TV and flapping its wings. I hardly even paid attention to it that first day. The next day when I came home from work I opened the door and every square centimeter of the place was covered with moths. I couldn't even see the floor or the curtains or the furniture. There must have been a million of them."

"Jesus," he said. Then, because he didn't know what else to say to that he repeated, "Jesus."

They both sat in the room with the anecdote, that kind of magic gaining special import in retrospect.

"How are your thumbs?" Greg asked, trying to focus them on a problem they could try to deal with.

"Fine," she said and laughed as she stuck up her thumbs, which looked wrinkled and weathered, like the hands of a woman much older. Jessica had a nervous habit of using her fingernails to peel back the skin of her thumbs when she was under stress and Greg knew the end of days would be hard on her digits.

"Oh my gods," he said in mock dismay. "It looks like you're holding two overcooked hot dogs."

She smiled, comfortable with the joke, if not the situation that prompted it.

They both stiffened when they heard the jeep arrive. The old, Malibu yellow one that Jessica's father had given to Cheyenne for her sixteenth birthday—the gift arriving conveniently after Jessica and her father had had one of their annual blowups. The jeep rattled to a stop in the driveway and Cheyenne entered and squinted her eyes at them before opening the closet in the hallway.

"Hey Cheyenne," Jessica said and then added another, unnecessary "Hi."

"Is that camera in here?" Cheyenne asked, removing scarves and boots from the closet. "The one that grandpa gave me for Christmas last year?"

Like most people from her age and income group demographic, Cheyenne did not use an actual camera, preferring instead the lower-megapixel, but more convenient option on her phone. The imminent day of reckoning, however, appeared to have made her sentimental.

"What do you need it for?" Greg asked, but she did not answer.

"How was the movie?" Jessica asked, trying to sound casual. Cheyenne yanked from the closet a milk crate full of wires and electrical cords Greg and Jessica had been acquiring since before they were married. Cheyenne sighed when the camera was not there either and put the crate back into the closet.

"Pretty bad. But there was this guy who was talking to us who was super-cute," she said, not looking up from the tangle of cords.

"What about Paul?" Jessica asked, continuing her ongoing inquiry into Cheyenne's relationship with the kid whose entire online existence seemed to include a skateboard and weed t-shirts. "Was Paul there?"

"Why do you always ask about Paul?" Cheyenne asked.

"Is Paul the boyfriend who won't come over here?" Greg asked.

"He's not my boyfriend." Cheyenne stood and struggled to close the door to the closet. "We are just messing around."

"Messing around how?" Jessica asked, the tone of her voice belying the shift of her line of questioning from rhetorical to interrogative.

"You guys are so dramatical. Maybe I'll just go live with Paul," she said. "Or my dad."

"You think you're going to live with your dad?" Greg asked.

"Greg," Jessica said, turning to look at him. She made her mouth small and tight, twisting her lips like a rag to silently remind Greg that they had agreed not to speak about Cheyenne's father until after the Metamorphosis. They had developed this silent communication style when they moved in together and had spent the last few years like two radio towers buzzing with information, vibrating with meaning from the centers of their complicated structures, but standing noiseless and stoic.

"I think that camera is in the basement," Jessica said, tossing the idea at both of them like a smoke bomb meant to distract. "I think I put it down there. But Greg is going to clean it out tomorrow, so he'll find it."

"Let me know when you have it," Cheyenne said, trotting up the steps to her room, careful not to run fast enough to reveal that she was retreating. Jessica turned toward Greg and made her eyes sharp.

"She's still mad about the move?" Greg asked.

"She's sixteen. She's mad about everything."

Holometabola (dramatical changes at the end of the cycle)

Greg found the camera the next day. It was sitting on an old miter-saw table in the middle of the basement as if it had been there all along, though he hadn't remembered ever seeing it there before. Under normal circumstances he would have just given the missing camera to Jessica, who seemed to have more access to Cheyenne, but Greg felt like there was power in the act of handing his stepdaughter the object she wanted, and the impending cataclysm made him want to tap into the sorcery of that kind of ritual.

Like most instances where magic is used without knowledge of its power, the exchange did not go as planned. Jessica heard Greg knock on Cheyenne's door and she also heard the brief interaction of her daughter and husband just before the escalation and eventual acrimonious eruption. The sound of their argument was like crickets drilling away in the distance, insistent and serrated.

"We don't have to talk about him anymore," Greg called, still carrying the camera he had intended to give to her, trying not to break it as he followed his stepdaughter's dramatic exit from the house. "Is this about the move?"

Jessica watched from the front room as the jeep sped wild and backward down the driveway and Greg followed. The jeep looked like a confused animal stung by a barb, scurrying away and wobbling with fear. Greg coasted down the driveway, his pursuit now a reflex, as Cheyenne turned the vehicle down the quiet, tree-lined street and pulled away, disappearing from view. Neighbors peered out from the windows of their home. The woman with six kids who had been sitting on her roof the day before looked at Greg from her front porch like he was already gone.

"Where did she go?" Greg asked when he came back inside, as if Jessica were the one who had just been speaking with Cheyenne.

"To Paul's, I assume," Jessica said. "Or maybe her dad's. But probably Paul's. She'll be back around 2 AM, probably."

"You think she'll drive all the way to Evanston?" he asked after a moment. It was the only thing he could think to say.

Jessica didn't answer. She picked at the skin on her thumbs, her jaw rippled as she tensed, and eventually she just looked out the window again. Greg realized he was still holding the camera. He placed it down on the coffee table before returning to the basement.

Ametabolan (no changes):

Jessica looked outside and saw that the sun was getting situated for the gloaming. She felt that sick feeling in the pit of her stomach that she used to get just before her father came home from work. She hadn't felt that way in years. The clock reported that it was well past noon and Jessica realized that she had slept through the big event.

She listened for Greg unloading the dishwasher, playing that keyboard in the basement, or doing God knows what in the bathroom, but she heard only silence. She imagined him in bed with her. She imagined the spell working its weird magic in reverse, those winged creatures coalescing to form her lover's body. She tried to convince herself that she didn't even really believe in the Metamorphosis anyway. That all these missing people were just hiding, maybe all in the same place, as some kind of sick joke.

But she did believe. Just like she believed in Comet Hale-Bopp and Y2K, and the end of the Mayan long calendar. Except she knew that this was real.

Jessica had known it might happen, that Greg might be gone, but she had not prepared herself. She opened the drawer where he kept his shoe polish, his stray picks, and the small wooden box where he kept his AA coin, his dark chocolate, and his cigarettes. It was Heather from her first home group who had told her, when Jessica was early in her own recovery, that dark chocolate helped with cravings. Jessica bit into it but it was stiff and chalky, so she spit it out and opted instead for the emergency pack of cigarettes that Greg did not know she knew about. She placed the cigarette in her mouth, too exhausted even to enjoy the fact that she didn't have to hide her tobacco use. She opened the bedroom door and descended the stairs. When she got to the first floor she smelled sausage, syrup, eggs, and coffee.

"They should make a t-shirt that says, 'I survived the Armageddon,'" Greg announced as Jessica came into the kitchen to find him cooking pancakes. "We're having breakfast for dinner because it's a special day. And also because it's the only thing I know how to cook." He stood in the kitchen, surrounded by pans, broken eggs, and Bisquick boxes. His smile was as broad and bright as the cherry on her cigarette. "Since when do you smoke?"

She was dazed. The cigarette, suddenly unimportant, dangled from her fingers.

"I prayed," she said quietly, as if saying it too loud might reverse the results of the prayer.

"Well, we made it," he said.

She wrapped her arms around him and cried, the sobs taking hold of her like an animal taking hold of prey. The cigarette fell to the floor. He held her for a moment and then kissed her on the top of her head, pulling away from their embrace to pick up the dropped cigarette and toss it, still smoking into the sink.

"Kinda puts everything into perspective, huh?" he said as he turned on the water to soak the cigarette. "With the move and everything. Things just work out sometimes."

And something about the way he said it made Jessica realize what had happened. She shuddered, called him a son of a bitch, and sprinted up the stairs to what was once her daughter's bedroom. She was so sure of what she would find that she didn't even bother knocking on the door.

The moths covered every square centimeter of the floor, the wings gently arcing against the air as if they had to move to keep from floating to the ceiling. And then they exited in a rush, filling the house like a sudden storm and then nothing. Emptiness filled the room and fouled everything in the half-lit space. The pictures on the wall. The empty bowls and plastic bags of candy. The clothes twisted in the corner like colorful ropes. The camera. They all had the distinct look of something abandoned.

Jessica thought back to the day before and tried to remember the last thing Cheyenne had said to her, but she couldn't recall. She tried to convince herself that she remembered. She tried to convince herself that it had been, "I'm sorry."

She heard Greg in the hallway, his steps shuffling and asymmetrical. He stopped in the doorway.

"She's gone." Jessica said it like an accusation.

"Did you hear her come back from Paul's? Or she could be at Melissa's. Or do you think she drove all the way to Evanston?"

"She's been transformed, Greg. But you already knew that."

"Jessica," he said. He sounded to Jessica like he was prepared for this accusation, and he was. He had been constructing his defense, building an argument that he knew would be airtight, but that he himself was not sure he believed. "Actually, if you want to compile a list of suspects for who would have wanted to get rid of her, we would be here all day. Teachers she was rude to, anyone who has ever shared the road with her. All of her ex-boyfriends. The cheerleading squad."

The open-handed slap didn't hurt, but it did stop him from talking. They stared at each other for so long that they had to shift their feet.

"I wasted my prayer on you," Jessica said, as if there was nothing left to say.

This conversation happened in households across the world. "Who did this to him?" and "Why did you choose her?" and "How could you think I would do that?"

In the ensuing months and years, support groups emerged where the messy parasites of survivor's guilt were addressed. Some refused to deal with or acknowledge the event. Some people even went out looking for the vanished, searching prisons and homeless shelters to see if they found a face they recognized. No one knew what to do or how to live in the aftermath of something like that.

Some groups tried to push for legislation to outlaw pesticides since their loved ones were now insects flying among the crops, but it was ultimately decided that progress couldn't be curtailed for something as difficult to determine as whether or not an insect had once been someone's brother, once been someone's lover, once been someone's mentor. And, anyway, we weren't sure exactly what had happened that day, were we? Were we?

There were experiments trying to compare existent insects to ones thought to have come into being after the metamorphoses, but the findings were vague and inconclusive. Theories about the cycle of such a transformation accumulated. Debates transpired about whether or not lifespans matched the bug, the transformed person, or somewhere in between. There was a lack of consensus on whether the people might turn back and whether they had turned at all.

No one used ant traps for a while. It almost ruined the industry. People started shooing moths and spiders out of their homes rather than squishing them, unsure which insects fell into which category. For a while it was not uncommon to find a bus driver out of his vehicle, standing in the street over the cracked-open body of a grasshopper, an accountant in a blouse and skirt crouched in the park over a stink bug, weeping during her lunch hour. For a while.

The world had been remade. Tyrants had been jettisoned, innocents had been martyred and there was no need to remove the bodies. It was simply time to move on. The post-apocalypse was far more polite and neat than anyone had imagined it would be. But, of course, the spots filled by those tyrants and martyrs wouldn't be vacant for long. While everyone argued over which entomic conversion was righteous and which was tragic, the world was recast anew, exactly as it was before.

Conclusions and Social Impact:

They'd decided not to move. Once Greg put in his two weeks' notice, his job matched the job offer from the company out of town, something he'd never considered, and so he turned down the offer from the new employer. They clung to what was familiar, their meetings, staring out at their neighbors, and watching Linda Carlisle on the news. The youthful newswoman was paired with a new co-anchor, one who looked suspiciously like his vanished predecessor, and Carlisle ominously reminded him and their viewers to be good to their families for the holidays and then she threw to commercial.

"So strange, huh?" Jessica said and tried to laugh.

"Weird," Greg agreed.

"What do you want to do about Christmas?" she asked him, as if it were a topic they were capable of discussing.

Greg looked up at the ceiling and exhaled, dreading the Christmas Eve dinner with Jessica's father and stepmother more than usual this year. The decision for the timing of the dinner had, in years previous, always been based around Cheyenne's schedule. Neither of them knew how to acknowledge this fact explicitly.

"Maybe we should talk to Gloria about it," she said before remembering only after she spoke that it would be impossible to ever talk to their marriage counselor again.

Greg tried to think of how to ask if he might be invited to her support group for the families of the Transformed but was afraid he might upset her. While they sat on the couch sighing and fidgeting, Jessica smashing the couch cushions out of the way and Greg nervously clasping and unclasping the battery cover of the remote control, they heard what sounded like a ten-year-old Malibu yellow jeep rattle to a stop in the driveway. They both held their breath, expecting her to burst into their living room, laughing about a guy she and Melissa saw at the mall who had gauges in his ears and who was super-cute. Jessica, for a moment, felt a sense of relief. She felt like maybe aborting the move had been the right decision, that she was right to assume Cheyenne would come back.

After a brief pause, she charged off the couch and opened the front door looking for the jeep, but no vehicle arrived. The sound of what they thought was an oncoming vehicle grew louder and more shrill until it seemed to change and become something else.

"Cicadas," Greg said. "It's just cicadas."

They saw the widower tottering around his single-level home, the wife of the guy who used to wash his truck every Saturday, the woman with five kids living in a two-bedroom bungalow, but they didn't see Jessica's daughter. They listened for the hum of cicadas for another moment until suddenly the buzz of it stopped and the sky was silent. They went back inside and returned to looking at the television, accepting the idea, all over again, that Cheyenne was gone.

ACKNOWLEDGMENTS

These stories would not be possible without the love, support, feedback, and ferocious criticism of the following people:

The Schenectadians, Matt Rector, Sarah Gray, Mike Feuerstein, Chris Aycox, and the late, great Noah Kucij.

The Southerners, Dan Leach and Stephen Hundley.

The Napervillians, Lou and Liz Holly, Laura Knapp, Jorge Busot, Alicia Burns, Jeremy Brown, Connor Hagen, Frank Fedele, Ray Ziemer, and Zarina Elahi.

The writers who keep me accountable, Christen Aragoni, Debbie Urbanski, Sarah Harwell, and Tina May Hall.

The editors who took an interest in the individual stories:

Cody Smith from *The Swamp*. Derek Askey, Carol Anne Fitzgerald, and Sy Safransky at *The Sun*. Erica Stisser from *Columbia Journal*. Erik Secker from *Bourbon Penn*. Valerie Vogrin, Geoff Schmidt, and Grant Deam at *Sou'Wester*, and Mal Smart from *Maudlin House*.

I am indescribably grateful to the endlessly patient and meticulously creative Siurong Ker, who found my book in a pile of other books and thought it was just weird enough.

Huzzah to the only creative writing teacher I ever had, Dr. Gregory Wolos who taught me an MFA's worth of knowledge in one semester at Schenectady High School.

To my shrinks. All of them. Even the bad ones. Especially the bad ones.

To my brother, despite/because of the fact that he won't read this. Writers need more people like that in their lives.

To Harvey and Stephanie, whom I love and who put up with me.

To my first reader and my last best hope, Jenny.

CREDITS

"A Painting of Such Reputation" was published in *ellipsis . . .*, Vol. 58, March 2022.

"The Southwest's Most Dangerous Babies" was published in *The Swamp*, Issue #4, February 2020.

"The Bedwetters" was published in SIU Edwardsville's *Sou'Wester*, Vol. 47, May 2019.

"Sunshowers" was published in *Columbia Journal Special Issue: EVOLVE 2018.*

"The Parts of a Shadow" was published in *Bourbon Penn*, Issue #16, October 2018.

"In Response to Your E-Newsletter Re: Peter Gabriel's Upcoming Summer Tour Dates" was published in *Maudlin House*, September 1, 2016.

"A Unified Conspiracy Theory" was published in *The Sun Magazine*, Issue #487, July 2016.

ABOUT THE AUTHOR

MATTHEW THOMAS MEADE has previously delivered newspapers, worked in a library, planted trees, and served coffee for a living, but he doesn't do any of those things anymore. His fiction has appeared in *The Sun Magazine*, *Bourbon Penn*, *The Saturday Evening Post*, and elsewhere. His chapbook, *Rocketflower*, won the C&R Press Summer Tide Pool Contest. Some of his work, as well as the one good picture he has of himself, can be found at www.matthewthomasmeade.com. Sometimes he has a mustache.

www.ingramcontent.com/pod-product-compliance
Ingram Content Group UK Ltd.
Pitfield, Milton Keynes, MK11 3LW, UK
UKHW041955190726
13854UKWH00005B/1978

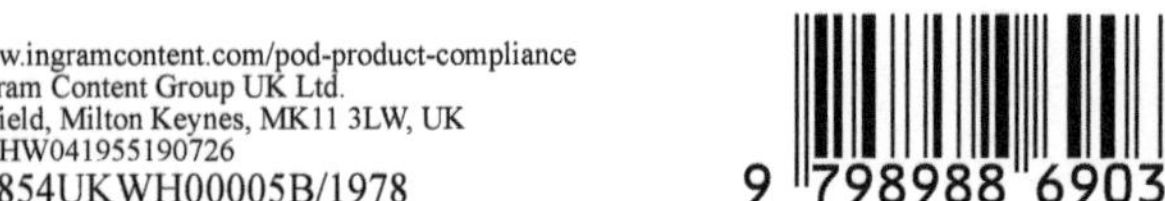

9 798988 690320